哈福

哈福

哈福

哈福

Three-Minute Shortcut to Best English

3分鐘
學會道地英語

用最短的時間　學最道地的英語

張瑪麗 ◎著

哈福

用最短的時間，學會最道地的英語

在美國，常有中國朋友痛苦地向我表示，和老美相交多年，為什麼語言上還是有隔閡，打不進他們的社交生意圈？

同樣的，國內也有許多朋友苦學英語多年，各式書籍、CD 買了一堆，補習費也沒少交，為何和老外講起話來仍是「雞同鴨講」，雙方一臉茫然？

有的英語課本和老師會建議你，如果外國朋友聽不懂你講的英語，就跟他們解釋這是台灣「特有的」。例如把補習班說成 cram school，外國人當然聽不懂。可是美國也有補習班，而且是連鎖的，規模很大。補習班的道地說法，請看本書第 82 句型。

注意，英語說得不道地，又要花許多口舌去解釋，只會被別人當成「異類」，失去很多交友經商的機會。

「入境隨俗」是每個人都知道的事，不先學會道地英語，如何讓老美對你另眼相看，稱兄道弟？

freshman 是九年級生還是大一新生？生病了要去 doctor's office 還是 hospital？老師說要做個 pop quiz，

提目是 multiple choice question 該怎麼辦？我們先去 drive-thru 餐廳，然後再去看 drive-in movie 是什麼意思？這些都是美國人日常生活中最典型的談話內容，何嘗不是我們自己的話題？

本書沒有困難的生字片語，都是中學就學過的英語。我們舉出中國人最容易犯的英語錯誤，告訴您最正確的說法，並列舉相關用語讓您舉一反三。

在「小秘訣」中，我們更用心地詳細分析中美文化的差異，和語言習慣的不同。舉凡日常生活語的食衣住行、社交應酬，各級學校學生的學習考試、交友應對，到上班族辦公室會話、人際關係等，都在本書範圍之內，務必使您在最短的時間之內，學到最道地的英語，享受和外國朋友打成一片、各得其利的樂趣。

您準備好了嗎？不要再羞於啟齒，勇敢向美國朋友大聲說出本書教您的「秘招」，保證他們立刻對您刮目相看，把你當做自己人看待，為您贏回應有的感情與尊重。

作者謹識

Contents

目錄

Contents

目錄

01 salary / paycheck

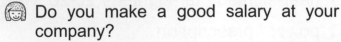

paycheck 就是上班族每個月領到的薪水

**MP3
02**

對話一

🎩 Do you make a good salary at your company?

（你在你公司的薪水高嗎？）

🤠 It's not bad.

（還好。）

對話二

🎩 Do you get paid on a salary or are you paid by the hour?

（你是領月薪的，還是計時算工資？）

🤠 I work for wages.

（我是計時算工資的。）

小秘訣

　　在台灣，上班族領薪水通常是領現金或由銀行轉帳，在美國是發一張 paycheck。所以你若告訴美國人你今天領到一包薪水袋 salary bag，對方可能會莫名其妙。你告訴他你今天領了 paycheck，那就不會有任何誤解了。

　　薪水有兩種算法，一種是算月薪，一種是計時算工資。領月薪的薪水英文用 salary，若是計時算工資的，英文用 wage，或是 by the hour。不過在美國說到 salary 是多少時，除非特別強調足月薪，否則指的是年薪，而不是月薪 (monthly salary)。

領 salary 的人，加班並沒有另外付錢。若是領 wage 的，也就是 paid by the hour 的，加班費是平常鐘點費的 1.5 倍。

salary 薪水

I am trying to get a raise in salary.
（我正在想辦法得到加薪。）

My salary doesn't go as far as it used to.
（我的薪水沒以前那麼多。）

I get my salary monthly.
（我領月薪。）

Does he make a good salary?
（他的薪水高嗎？）

paycheck 薪水支票；薪水袋

My paycheck is not much this week.
（我這星期領到的薪水不多。）

I don't like living from paycheck to paycheck.
（我不喜歡靠領薪水過日子。）

I'll trade my paycheck for yours.
（我可以跟你交換薪水袋。）

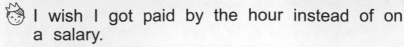

paid by the hour 計時算工資

I wish I got paid by the hour instead of on a salary.

（我希望我是計時算工資，而不是領月薪。）

Do you get paid time and a half for overtime?

（你加班費有沒有 1 倍半？）

▶ wages 工資

The clerk works for wages.

（這職員是計時算工資。）

▶ pay 付錢（本課做付薪水的意思）

The job pays ten thousand dollars a week.

（這工作每星期的工資是一萬元。）

I'll take the job at the gift shop. Because it pays more.

（我接受了在禮品屋的工作，因為那家付的薪水比較高。）

單字片語

- make a good salary 領高薪
- trade 以物易物
- time and a half 一倍半（1.5 倍）
- overtime 加班
- salary ['sælərɪ] 薪水

02 part-time/full-time

part-time 是兼職，full-time 是上全職班

對話一

Do you work full-time or part-time?

（你是全職還是兼職的？）

I work full-time.

（我是上全職班。）

Is that 40 hours a week?

（一個星期是不是 40 小時？）

I work a lot of overtime, so it is usually more like 50 hours.

（我常加班，所以通常是 50 小時左右。）

對話二

Does he have a full-time job?

（他有全職的工作嗎？）

No, he only works part-time on the weekends.

（不，他只在週末兼差。）

小秘訣

　　part-time 和 full-time 這兩個字，可以當副詞也可以當形容詞。當副詞用時如：兼職工作 work part-time，當形容詞用時如：全職的工作 full-time job。至於說某人是兼職工作的人，則是 part-timer。

full-time 全職上班

👦 Do you like working full-time?
（你喜歡全職上班嗎？）

👦 Does she have a full-time job?
（她有個全職的工作嗎？）

👦 What are the benefits of full-time employment?
（全職班有什麼福利？）

part-time 兼職

👦 I am looking for a part-time job.
（我在找一份兼職的工作。）

👦 I work a part-time job for extra income.
（我兼職工作，多賺一點錢。）

👦 He won't know the answer. He is only a part-timer.
（他不會知道答案，他只是兼職人員。）

overtime 加班

👦 How much overtime did you work last week?
（你上星期加班多少小時？）

👦 She is a workaholic--she worked 30 hours overtime last week.

（她是工作狂－－她上星期加了 30 小時的班。）

 I'm trying to work overtime so I can buy a new car.
（我正想辦法加班，以便可以買部新車。）

 單字片語

- benefit ['bɛnəfɪt] 福利

- employment [ɪm'plɔɪmənt] 雇用

- workaholic [ˌwɝkə'hɑlɪk] 工作狂

- look for 尋找

03 work/job

work 和 job 中文都翻譯成工作，鄰是兩種性質不同的工作

MP3 04

對話一

 I'm looking for a new job.
（我在找一份新工作。）

 Doing what?
（做什麼的？）

 The same thing, but at a different place.
（做同樣的事情，但是在不同的地方。）

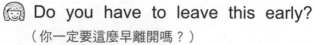 Good luck.
（祝你成功。）

對話二

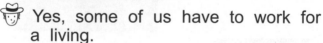 Do you have to leave this early?
（你一定要這麼早離開嗎？）

 Yes, some of us have to work for a living.
（是的，我們當中有人必須為生活而工作。）

I work just as hard as you.
（我跟你一樣努力工作的。）

 I doubt that.
（我不相信。）

work 和 job 中文都翻譯成工作，卻是兩種性質不同的工作 work 和 job 中文都翻譯成工作，但從以上兩個對話可以清楚的看出兩個字的不同。job 是指一份職業，例如：a new job 一份新的工作；work 則是指做事情，例如：He works very hard.（他很努力工作。）

work 指做事情，可以當名詞和動詞。當名詞：a lot of work（很多工作）。當動詞：work very hard（很努力工作）。

work 除了當「做事情」外，還可以指上班做事，做名詞和動詞都行。當名詞：What kind of work are you in?（你上班做什麼工作？）；當動詞 He works in a law firm.（他在一家律師事務所上班。）

job 工作（指一份職業）

What kind of job are you looking for?
（你在找什麼樣的工作？）

Are you having any luck finding a job?
（你找工作順利嗎？）

She quit her job because she hated it.
（她辭職了，因為她不喜歡那工作。）

work: 工作（指做事情或上班做事）

▶ 做事情

He doesn't know what hard work is.
（他不知道什麼叫做努力工作。）

Taking care of a baby requires a lot of work.
（照顧一個嬰兒要花很多工夫。）

▶ 上班做事

Does your mom work?
（你的母親有上班嗎？）

Mother's work is in the home.
（母親的工作是在家裏。）

What kind of work are you in?
（你上班做什麼工作？）

What kind of work does your father do?
（你父親是做什麼的？）

 單字片語

- ✪ doubt [daʊt] v. 懷疑

- ✪ I doubt that. 我不相信（是一句口語）

- ✪ quit [kwɪt] v. 停止（動詞三態：quit, quit, quit）

- ✪ require [rɪ'kwaɪr] v. 要求

04 office/work

my office 是指我們公司，go to work 是去上班

MP3 05

對話一

Are you going to work today?
（你今天要去上班嗎？）

No, I have the day off.
（不，我今天休假。）

My office never lets me have a day off.
（我們公司從不讓我休假。）

Maybe you should work somewhere else.
（或許你該到別的地方去上班。）

對話二

How long have you been with this company?
（你在這家公司上班多久了？）

About 12 years.
（大約 12 年。）

Wow, you must really enjoy your job.
（哇，你一定很喜歡你的工作。）

Most of the time I like my work.
（大部份時間我是蠻喜歡我的工作。）

小秘訣

　　平常提到我們公司或你們公司，用 my office，your office 就行。
這裡所說的公司，主要是指上班的地方。若是句中是指上班的「公司」時，還是要用 company，例如：I make a good salary at my company.。

office 辦公室（在本課指公司）

Your office called and said they needed you to come in.
（你的公司打電話來說他們要你過去。）

Does your office allow smoking?
（你們公司可以抽煙嗎？）

Why don't you call in sick to your office?
（你為何不打電話到公司請病假？）

▶ company 公司

My father works for a computer company.
（我父親在一家電腦公司上班。）

A new company has just been formed in our town.
（我們鎮上剛成立一家新公司。）

work 上班

She works in a law firm.
（她在一家律師事務所上班。）

We all need to get to work.
（我們都必須上班。）

I don't feel like going to work today.
（我今天不想去上班。）

I came home sick from work today.
（我今天上班時請病假回家。）

單字片語

- company [ˈkʌmpənɪ] 公司
- call in sick 打電話去請病假
- have a day off 休假一天

05 work on/work for

work on 是要特別花工夫去做的事；
work for 是在某處上班

MP3
06

對話一

 How is Mary ?

（瑪麗怎麼樣？）

 I don't know.

（還不知道。）

The doctor is still working on her.

（醫生正在醫治她。）

I hope she'll be all right.

（我希望她沒事。）

對話二

 Who do you work for?

（你替誰做事？）

 I work for a small insurance
company.

（我在一家小保險公司上班。）

小秘訣

　　work on 是指特別花工夫去做某事，例如：醫生 work on 一個病人，
指醫生正在醫治病人；work on a project 就是去做一個企劃。

　　work for 的介系詞 for 指「替誰工作」；也就是在哪兒上班的意思。
Who do you woke for? 的 Who 是介系詞 for 的受詞，理論上應該用
Whom，但口語上美國人都習慣於用 Who，用 Whom 反而顯得太文
謅謅。

work on 花時間做某事

I have to work on this project tonight.
（我今晚一定要做這個企劃。）

She is supposed to be working on her homework.
（她應該要做她的家庭作業。）

The doctor is still working on your mother. There is no news yet.
（醫生還在醫治你的母親，還沒有消息。）

work for 替～做事（在哪裡上班）

Who does he work for?
（他在哪裡上班？）

Who were you working for then?
（你那時替誰工作？）

單字片語

- insurance [ɪnˈʃʊrəns] 保險
- insurance company 保險公司
- project [ˈprɑdʒɛkt] 企劃
- be supposed to~ 應該～

06 colleague/co-worker

同事；伙伴。colleague 這個單字不好背，co-worker 也可以

MP3 07

對話一

 Someone I work with suggested I try this restaurant.

（有同事建議我試試這家餐廳。）

 Really? Someone in my office told me it was good, too.

（真的？我們公司也有人說這家很好。）

對話二

 How do you get along with your co-workers?

（你跟同事相處得如何？）

 I get along well with most of them.

（我跟大部份的同事相處得不錯。）

小秘訣

　　若問「同事」的英文該怎麼說，那非 colleague 這個字莫屬了。但是這個字既不好背也不好唸，當你提到同事時，用 co-worker，someone I work with 或 someone in my office 都是正確、明瞭的說法。

colleague 同事

Sarah and I have been colleagues for years.
（莎拉和我同事多年了。）

I don't consider him a colleague of mine anymore since we stopped working together.
（我們已經不再一起工作，所以我不認為他是我的同事。）

co-worker 同事

One of my co-workers quit today.
（今天有一個同事辭職了。）

How many co-workers do you have in your company?
（你的公司員工有多少人？）

My boss fired one of my co-workers today.
（我的老闆今天辭掉一位同事。）

I wish you would tell me which of my co-workers to invite to the party.
（我希望你能告訴我應該邀請哪些同事來宴會。）

▶ someone in my office 公司同仁；同事

Did someone in your office tell you I called today?
（你們公司的同事告訴你，我今天打過電話嗎？）

I think someone in your office is telling company secrets.

（我認為你們公司有人在洩露公司的秘密。）

▶ someone I work with 公司同仁；同事

Someone I work with has a crush on our boss.

（有一位同事愛上我們老闆。）

Someone I work with told me a joke.

（有位同事講了個笑話給我聽。）

 單字片語

- restaurant [ˈrɛstərənt] 餐廳
- colleague [ˈkɑlig] 同事
- get along with ～ 與～相處
- secret [ˈsikrɪt] 秘密

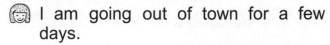

07 out of town on business

out of town 只是到外地去；出差是 out of town on business

MP3 08

對話一

 I am going out of town for a few days.

（我要外出幾天。）

Are you going on vacation?

（是去度假嗎？）

 No, I'm going on a business trip.

（不是，是去出差。）

對話二

I have to go out of town on business this week.

（我這個星期要到外地去。）

 Where are you going?

（你要去哪裏？）

小秘訣

出差有好幾種説法：go out of town on business, go on a business trip, go away on business 和 do business travel 都是沒説明目的

地，只説要去出差。而 take a business trip to 某地，go to 某地 on business，則説明了要去某地方出差。

　　take a business trip to（做某事），則是説明了出差目的。

out of town 到外地去

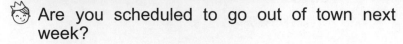 Are you scheduled to go out of town next week?

（你安排好下星期要到外地去嗎？）

▶ out of town on business 去出差

She had to go out of town on business.

（她必須去出差。）

Do you go out of town on business often?

（你常出差嗎？）

▶ business trip 商務旅行（出差）

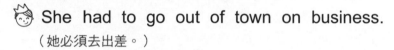 I am taking a business trip to Portland.

（我要到波特蘭出差。）

They are planning a business trip to meet the President of the company.

（他們正計劃出差去和公司總裁見面。）

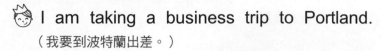 I haven't done a lot of business travel lately.

（我最近很少做商務旅行。）

I am going to Chicago on business.

（我要去芝加哥出差。）

My husband goes away on business a lot.

（我先生常出差。）

This is not a pleasure trip. I am away on business.

（這不是去玩。是去談生意。）

I am away on business almost all the time.

（我一天到晚出差。）

 單字片語

- schedule [ˈskɛdʒul]　預定
- pleasure [ˈplɛʒɚ]　娛樂

08 vacation/holiday

聖誕節是 holiday，春假是 spring break，兩者都不是 vacation

MP3 09

對話一

 Do you think the beaches will be crowded over the holidays?

（你想假期中海邊會不會很擁擠？）

 It sure will, especially during the three day weekend.

（一定會的，尤其是長週末。）

對話二

 Have you taken your vacation this year yet?

（你今年休假請完了沒？）

 No, but I'll be on vacation starting next week.

（還沒，但我從下星期起開始休假。）

小秘訣

vacation 是休假，指公司給的休假。這跟請假不一樣，請假是臨時性的，休假要事先跟公司安排時間，休假並不一定要出去玩，在家裏沒事，也是在 on vacation。

休假時間的長短，每個公司政策不同，跟職位的高低也有關。

如果你是上班族，美國朋友問你何時有 vacation，碰巧新年快到了，

你回答説「快了」I'll have a New Year vacation.，或是春假快到了，你回答説 I'll have a spring vacation next week. 非把你的美國朋友弄得啼笑皆非不可。記住，新年是一個 holiday，春假是 spring break，兩者都不是 vacation。

　　holiday 是假日或節日，例如：端午節、中秋節、雙十節、新年、聖誕節、感恩節等。

　　break 是指一段時間的休息，這時間可長可短，可以是 5 分鐘的 break, 也可以像春假 5 天的 break。

　　on vacation 可以指度假，或是指不上班在休假中。take one's vacation 就是把公司應給的休假時間用掉，卻不是請假。請假是 take a day off，請病假是 take a sick day。

vacation 休假

▶ take one's vacation 休假

Aren't you taking a vacation soon?
（你快要休假了嗎？）

I've taken my vacation this year.
（我今年的休假已經請完了。）

I'm going to take my vacation next week.
（我下星期要休假。）

I took my vacation last week.
（我上星期休假。）

on vacation: 去度假;在休假中

▶ 去度假

We haven't been on vacation in years.
（我們已經好幾年沒去度假了。）

Where are you going on vacation this year?
（今年你們要去哪裏度假？）

▶ 在休假中

I'll be away on vacation for three weeks.
（我將休假三個星期。）

▶ summer vacation 暑假

（跟上班族無關,是學生的專利,要用 vacation 這個字）

Our summer vacation lasts three months.
（我們暑假長達三個月。）

holiday 假日;節日

Are you going out of town over the Christmas holidays?
（聖誕假期中,你要外出嗎？）

I am going to visit my relatives over the holidays.
（假期中,我要去拜訪我的親戚。）

I am looking forward to resting during the three day holiday.

（我期待在三天假期中好好休息。）

Thanksgiving is a holiday in all States.

（感恩節是全美國的假日。）

 Easter is a Christian holiday.

（復活節是基督教的節日。）

break 休息

You may take a five-minute break.

（你可以休息 5 分鐘。）

Spring break starts on April 2.

（春假從 4 月 2 日開始。）

 單字片語

- ○ vacation [veˈkeʃən] 休假
- ○ holiday [ˈhɑləˌde] 假日；節日
- ○ last [læst] v. 持續
- ○ look forward to ～ 期待～
- ○ relative [ˈrɛlətɪv] 親戚

09 long weekend

長週末，就是星期五、或星期一也放假的週末

MP3
10

小秘訣

在美國每週上五天班，星期六和星期日不上班，所以從星期五下班後到星期日晚上為止都是 weekend（週末）。但有時遇到星期五或星期一也放假時，就會有一連三天或四天的週末，所以，叫 long weekend 或 three day weekend。

weekend 週末

We went out of town for the weekend.
（我們週末到外地去。）

John works part-time on the weekends.
（約翰在週末做兼職的工作。）

▶ three day weekend 三天的週末

What are you going to do over the three day weekend?
（你這三天的週末要做什麼？）

 Are you taking a trip over the long weekend?

（這個長週末你要去旅行嗎？）

 單字片語

- ☉ weekend ['wik'ɛnd] 週末
- ☉ take a trip 旅行

10 take a sick leave/take a day off

vacation 不包括請，請假是 take a day off

對話一

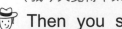 I don't feel well today.

（我今天覺得不太舒服。）

Then you should call in sick to work.

（那你應該打電話去請假。）

I can't. I have too much to do.

（不行，我有很多事要做。）

Yes, but, you're sick.

（沒錯，但是，你在生病啊。）

對話二

I think I am going to take the day off.

（我想我要請一天假。）

You should. You have been working too hard lately.

（應該的，你最近做得太辛苦了。）

小秘訣

　　請病假通常是當天早上覺得不舒服，才決定請假的，所以最常見的英語是 call in sick（打電話請病假）。你告訴別人說你請了病假，英語是 I took a sick day. 或 I took a sick leave.。有些特殊情況，例

如要動手術，是可以事先安排的，那就說 I'm going to take（幾天）of sick leave.（我要請幾天病假），至於天數，你可以填 two days，three days 或 two weeks, {ks，} three weeks。

若單純說請假，沒特別指名是請什麼假，就說 take a day off，或 take the day off。

call in sick 打電話請病假

He called in sick this morning.
（他今早打電話來請病假。）

She called in sick again today.
（她今天又打電話來請病假。）

I don't like calling in sick to work.
（我不喜歡打電話去請病假。）

take a sick day 請一天病假

I took a sick day from work.
（我請了一天病假。）

He isn't coming in today due to illness.
（他病了，今天不會來。）

▶ take a sick leave 請病假

I'm going to take two days of sick leave.
（我將要請兩天病假。）

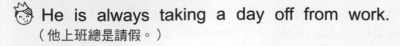

take a day off 請一天假

He is always taking a day off from work.
（他上班總是請假。）

I need to take a day off and get away from everything.
（我需要請一天假，遠離一切。）

take the day off 請假（談話者彼此知道是說哪一天）

You should call in sick and take the day off.
（你應該打電話去請個病假。）

I took the day off yesterday.
（我昨天請假。）

▶ have time off 有假期

I have time off in early September. I'm going to Europe for a trip.
（我九月初有假期，我要去歐洲旅行。）

 單字片語

- ◎ leave [liv] 請假

- ◎ illness [ˈɪlnɪs] 生病

- ◎ Europe [ˈjʊrəp] 歐洲

- ◎ September [sɛpˈtɛmbɚ] 九月

36

11 sick/ill

生病時用 sick 或 ill 都行

MP3
12

對話一

 Why didn't you come to school yesterday?

（你昨天為何沒來上學？）

I was sick.

（我病了。）

對話二

 She has not been in good health lately.

（她最近身體一直不太好。）

I know. She never seems to feel well.

（我知道，她似乎一直都不太舒服。）

小秘訣

　說到生病，用 ill 或 sick 都可以，理論上 ill 是較正式的説法。以上例句中，B 回答我病了 I was sick.，也可以説 I was ill.。

　如果要説明生什麼病，例如，感冒了或發燒了，就加個介系詞 with, 例如：be sick with the flu, be ill with a cold。

生病不一定要用 be 動詞，也可以用 take，例如：I took sick with a cold. 或 I took ill.。

ill 只當生病的意思。sick 除了生病的意思外，還可以指胃不舒服想吐，例如：get sick。也可已指對某事很厭煩或覺得受不了，例如：I'm sick of the noise.（我受不了那噪音。）。

sick 病了

Mary is sick with the flu.
（瑪麗患了流行性感冒。）

Mary is ill with a bad cold.
（瑪麗患了重感冒。）

▶ take sick 生病

I took sick with a bad cold last week.
（我上星期患了重感冒。）

I hope I don't take ill before final exams.
（我希望期末考之前，我別生病）

▶ get sick 胃不舒服想吐

Mary often gets sick from riding in the car.
（瑪麗常會暈車。）

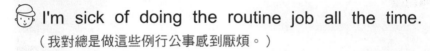

▶ be sick of 受不了；厭煩

I'm sick of doing the routine job all the time.

（我對總是做這些例行公事感到厭煩。）

ill 病了

Mary didn't come to work because she was ill with a cold.

（瑪麗沒有來上班，因為她感冒了。）

He has been ill for several weeks.

（他已經病了好幾個星期。）

 單字片語

- ❂ flu [flu] 流行性感冒
- ❂ ride [raɪd] 乘；坐（車子）
- ❂ final ['faɪnl] 最後的
- ❂ routine [ru'tin] 例行公事
- ❂ all the time 總是

12 feel well/in good health

in good health 是形容詞片語，指身體健康

 小秘訣

　　說身體健康要用 feel well，不說 feel good，因為 well 當形容詞是指身體健康的意思。而 feel 是連綴動詞，後面要加形容詞來形容主詞。

feel well 身體健康

 I don't feel well.
（我覺得不舒服。）

I haven't felt well this week.
（我這個星期都不舒服。）

in good health 身體健康

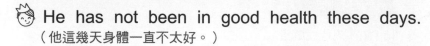 He has not been in good health these days.
（他這幾天身體一直不太好。）

 He is in very good health.
（他的身體很健康。）

 單字片語

　⊙ health [hɛlθ] 健康

13 catch a cold/had a cold

感冒了到底是要用 catch a cold，還是 had a cold 呢？

對話一

 You'd better watch out. The flu is going around.

（你最好小心，流行性感冒正在流行。）

 I know. Mary didn't come to work because she had a cold.

（我知道，瑪麗沒有來上班，因為她病了。）

對話二

 It's cold outside. Aren't you putting on the coat?

（外面很冷，你不穿外套嗎？）

 No, I'm fine.

（不用，沒關係的）

 You'd better put on the coat or you'll catch a cold.

（你最好把外套穿上，否則你會感冒的。）

cold（感冒）若要用 catch 這個動詞，只用在現在式或未來式。例如 You'll catch a cold.（你會感冒的），或 I catch a cold every year at this time.（我每年這時候，都會感冒），注意：每年都發生的事用現在式。

要說「我感冒了」要用 I had a cold，若說 I caught a cold. 在文法上是沒錯，但美國人不這麼說。

至於 flu（流行性感冒）可以用 get 或 have 這兩個動詞，例如：I got the flu. 或 I had the flu.（我患了流行感冒）。美國人不會說 You'll catch the flu.。

catch a cold 感冒

Be careful not to catch a cold.

（小心別感冒了。）

Please close the window, or we'll catch cold.

（請把窗戶關上，否則我們會感冒的。）

I catch a cold every year at this time.

（每年這時候我都會感冒。）

have a cold 感冒

Mary was absent from school because she had a cold.

（瑪麗沒來上學因為她感冒了。）

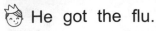 He got the flu.
（他患了流行性感冒。）

 She is in bed with the flu.
（她感冒在床。）

I think you have the flu that's been going around.
（我想你是得了正在流行的流行性感冒。）

 單字片語

- ○ watch out 小心
- ○ had better 最好
- ○ put on 穿上
- ○ absent [ˈæbsn̩t] 缺席的

看醫生不一定要到醫院去

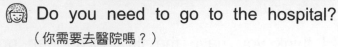

MP3
15

對話一

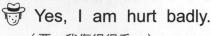 Do you need to go to the hospital?

（你需要去醫院嗎？）

Yes, I am hurt badly.

（要，我傷得很重。）

對話二

Where is your doctor's office?

（你的醫生診所在哪裏？）

It is on Main Street next to my office.

（在我公司旁的緬因街上。）

What time is your appointment?

（你約好幾點去看醫生？）

2:00 p.m.

（下午 2 點。）

小秘訣

在美國看醫生都是在 doctor's office，所以中文說去看醫生，可以說 go to see a doctor，也可以說 go to the doctor's office，卻不說 go to the hospital。因為 hospital 是生大病、受重傷需要動

44

手術或治療時才去的。雖然有的 doctor's office 是設在 hospital 內，但你還是去 doctor's office，而不是去 hospital。

hospital 醫院

▶ hospital 醫院

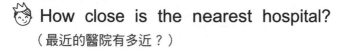 How close is the nearest hospital?
（最近的醫院有多近？）

Is St. Thomas a good hospital?
（聖湯姆斯醫院是一家好的醫院嗎？）

▶ in the hospital 住院

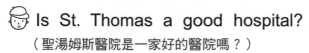 She is in the hospital having her tonsils removed.
（她住院要拿掉扁桃腺。）

How long were you in the hospital when you gave birth?
（你生產時住院多久？）

doctor's office 醫生診所

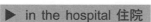 Your doctor's office called today.
（你的醫生診所今天打電話來。）

What time is your appointment at the doctor's office?

（你跟醫生約好幾點？）

If this cold gets worse, I will have to go to the doctor's office.

（如果感冒惡化的話，我就必須去看醫生。）

I am looking for a doctor's office near my home.

（我在找一位離我家近一點的醫生。）

 單字片語

- hospital [ˈhɑspɪtḷ] 醫院

- hurt [hɝt] 受傷

- appointment [əˈpɔɪntmənt] 約會

- look for ～ 尋找～

15 get a check-up/check into the hospital

住院，做健康檢查

小秘訣

　　一般說某人住院，英文是（某人）is in the hospital。但若只是打算要住院時，不是說（某人）will be in the hospital，而是說（某人）is checking into the hospital。

　　送某人去住院，不是 send（某人）to the hospital，而是 check（某人）into the hospital。平時不生病時也應該定期做健康檢查，英文是 get a check-up。

check into the hospital　要住院

 I am checking into the hospital tomorrow.
（我明天要去住院。）

 They checked him into the hospital last night.
（他們昨晚把他送去住院。）

get a check-up 做個健康檢查

 My father is going to have a check-up in the morning. I hope he's okay.

（我父親明天早上要去做健康檢查，我希望他沒事。）

give someone a check-up 替某人做健康檢查

 The doctor gave John a check-up.

（醫生替約翰做健康檢查。）

 單字片語

- ❂ doctor [ˈdɑktɚ] 醫生

16 college/university

上大學說 go to college，或是 go to university 都可以

MP3 17

對話一

What college did you attend?
（你上哪一所大學？）

I went to Washington University.
（我上華盛頓大學。）

I've never heard of that.
（我沒聽說過那所大學。）

It is in Wyoming.
（那是在懷俄明州。）

對話二

My university wants me to speak at a luncheon.
（我們學校要我在午餐會上演講。）

Wow, that's an honor.
（哇，那是一項榮譽呢！）

小秘訣

上大學到底應該說 go to college，還是說 go to university 呢？理

論上 college 是學院，綜合好幾個 college 而成立一所 university。有一天，我與朋友上高三的女兒在談她要去上大學的事情，談話中每次說到上大學，我都是說 go to college，女孩的媽媽忍不住向我抗議，說我女兒是要去 university，而不是要去 college。實際上，美國人說大學，用 college 或 university 都可以。但因為 university 音節太長，美國人在談話中，多用 college。

如果是提到大學名稱時，因為每一所大學有其固定的名稱，就不可以把 college 和 university 隨便混用。例如 California University，就不可叫該校 California College，該校若叫做 New York College，你不可稱它為 New York University。

university 大學

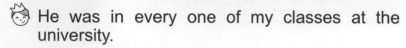 He was in every one of my classes at the university.

（大學時，他每一科都跟我同班。）

I think your university is more expensive than mine.

（我認為你們學校比我們學校貴。）

What courses are you taking at the university?

（你在大學裏修哪些課？）

college 大學

Which college are you going to go?
（你要去上哪一所大學？）

I'm going to college next fall.
（我明年秋天要去上大學。）

He dropped out of college.
（他退學了。）

Did you like your college professors?
（你喜歡你的大學教授嗎？）

單字片語

- college [ˈkɑlɪdʒ] 大學
- attend [əˈtɛnd] 參加
- university [junəˈvɝsətɪ] 大學
- luncheon [ˈlʌntʃən] 午餐會

17 grade/year

從小學一年級到高三有 12 個 grades，大學則有 4 個 years

對話一

What grade is your son in now?
（你兒子現在幾年級了？）

He is in the 6th grade.
（他讀六年級。）

Wow, he is really growing up.
（哇，他真是長大了。）

Yes, he is.
（是啊。）

對話二

I am in my 3rd year of college and I still don't know what my major should be.
（我已經大三了，但我仍然不知道該主修什麼。）

Don't worry. You'll figure it out.
（別擔心，你會知道的。）

小秘訣

說到學校的年級，以美國的學制而言，從小學一年級到高三畢業都用 grade 這個字，因為們是從 1st grade 直到 12th grade.

52

全美各州可自訂學年，有些學區初一是 **6th grade**；有些區初一是 **7th grade**。所以你要告訴美國人你是唸初一時，最好說 **7th grade**。你若告訴美國人你是 first year in the junior high，對方仍不能確定你到底是 6 年級還是 7 年級。

從 9 年級到 12 年級，也可說是 freshman year, sophomore year, junior year 和 senior year，跟四年制大學的說法一樣。所以如果有美國中學生告訴你他是 sophomore，你可別以為他是在唸大學。事實上，他是唸 10 年級，等於台灣的高一。

說到大學的年級，不是用 grade 而用 year。例如 I'm in my 3rd year of college。

grade 年級

My sister is in the 5th grade.
（我妹妹在唸 5 年級。）

I skipped ahead two grades when I was in school.
（我唸書時，跳了兩個年級。）

What grade are you in?
（你是幾年級的？）

▶ grader （幾）年級生

My sister is a sixth grader.
（我妹妹是 6 年級。）

My sophomore year was the hardest for me.
（高二那一年對我而言最困難。）

（這裡的 sophomore year 也可以指大二。）

What year in college are you?
（你是大學幾年級？）

I skipped a lot of classes of my senior year in high school.
（我高三時蹺很多課。）

I am in my 3rd year of Spanish.
（我正在修第 3 年的西班牙文。）

How many years of Chemistry did you take?
（你修了幾年的化學？）

 單字片語

○ grade [gred] 年級

○ grow up 長大

○ figure out [ˈfɪgjɚ aʊt] 瞭解；知道

○ Chemistry [ˈkɛmɪstrɪ] 化學

18 freshman

9 年級生和大一學生都是新鮮人

小秘訣

　　大一學生是 freshman，大二是 sophomore，大三是 junior，大四是 senior。在美國從 9 年級到 12 年級生，也就是初三到高三，也是叫做 freshman, sophomore, junior 和 senior。

　　那麼，若有人提到 freshman year，到底應該是初三還是大一呢？一般來說，從大家正在談話的內容應該可以知道，是在說初三那一年還是大一那一年。若還是不清楚，你也可以問到底是 freshman year in high school，還是 freshman year in college。

 ## 單字片語

- ☺ freshman [ˈfrɛʃmən] 新鮮人；大一；9 年級
- ☺ sophomore [ˈsɑfəmor] 大二；10 年級
- ☺ junior [ˈdʒunjɚ] 大三；11 年級
- ☺ senior [ˈsinjɚ] 大四；12 年級

score/grade

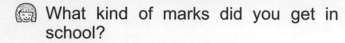

score 和 grade 都是成績，只是評定方式不同

MP3
20

對話一

 What kind of marks did you get in school?

（你在學校的成績如何？）

 I made very good grades.

（我的成績很好。）

對話二

 What was your score on the test?

（這次測驗你考幾分？）

 I made 96 out of 100 points.

（我考 96 分。）

小秘訣

　　學業成績的評定有好幾種方式，若是以 A、B、C 或是甲、乙、丙來打成績，英文就是 grade 或 mark。若是以 92 分、98 分、70 分……等來給成績，那就該用 score。但是 score 是指得到的總分，例如：My score on the math test was 89.（我的數學是 89 分）。如果答錯一題要扣 5 分，要說 five points，而不是 five scores。

　　你告訴你的美國朋友你考了 98 分，對方可能不知道你考了高分。在台灣，我們的滿分總是以 100 分來算，但在美國，滿分可能是200 分，甚至是 600 分。為了讓對方知道你考了很高分，你可以說

I made 98 out of 100 points.。若是美國人告訴你 I made a perfect score. 是說他得到滿分，但不一定是 100 分，但在台灣一般的考試 perfect score 就是 100 分了。

grade 等級；成績

His grades are mostly B's.
（他的成績大部分是 B。）

I made a bad grade.
（我的成績考得不好。）

I don't care about making good grades.
（我不在乎考好成績。）

▶ 打分數；給成績

The teacher is grading the papers.
（老師在打報告的分數。）

The teacher is marking the literature papers.
（老師在打文學報告分數。）

The teacher is scoring the math test.
（老師在算數學測驗的分數。）

mark 等級；成績

His dad said he would buy him a car if he made good marks.
（他的父親說如果他得到好成績的話，就要買車子給他。）

She got a mark of B in spelling.
（她的拼字成績是 B。）

His mark in spelling was C.
（他拼字成績是 C。）

score 總得分

Mary made a perfect score on her test.
（瑪麗考了滿分。）

My score on the spelling test was 78.
（我的拼字測驗考了 78 分。）

What was your score on English test?
（你的英文考幾分？）

 單字片語

- ☺ make good grades 得到好成績
- ☺ make good marks 得到好成績

20 score/point

point 的分數加起來就是 score

對話一

 How is our team doing?
（我們這隊打得怎麼樣？）

The score is 30 to 20. We are ahead by 10 points.
（比數是 30 比 20，我們領先 10 分。）

小秘訣

　　球類比賽每次的得分是 point，例如籃球進籃得了 5 個 points，棒球全壘打得了 4 個 points，我們隊領先 7 個 points。得到的 points 加起來就是 score。例如：我們的籃球隊目前的 score 是 78 分。考試得到的總分是 score，每一題幾分是 point，若是每一題 5 points，錯了兩題，要扣 10 points，得到的總分 score 是 90 分。

score 總得分

▶ 比數

 The score is 2 to 1.
（比數是 2 比 1。）

▶ 得分（當動詞）

 John scored twenty points in the basketball game.
（約翰在籃球比賽得了 20 分。）

What was your score on the math test?
（你的數學考幾分？）

point 每次的分數

A touchdown is worth 6 points.
（足球賽每一次觸地得分是 6 分。）

Our basketball team is ahead by 20 points.
（我們的籃球隊領先 20 分。）

The teacher took off points because my paper was late.
（因為我的報告遲交，老師扣了分數。）

I got bonus points on my test.
（我的考試成績得到額外的加分。）

成績

What did you make in History?
（你的歷史考幾分？）

What did she get on her test?
（她考試考幾分？）

 單字片語

- score [skor] 總得分

- point [pɔɪnt] 分

21 place/prize

place 是得到名次，得 prize 是得獎

MP3 22

對話一

How did your painting do?

（你的油畫怎麼樣？）

It took first place in the contest.

（在比賽中得了第一名。）

Wow, that's great.

（哇，太棒了。）

Yes, I'm very proud.

（是啊，我也覺得很光榮。）

對話二

Did you hear that she got an award for her poem?

（你有沒有聽說她的詩得獎了？）

That's wonderful.

（那太棒了。）

小秘訣

比賽名次英文用 place。第一名是 first place，第二名 second place，第三名 third place，依此類推。得名的動詞可以用 take、get 或 win。

比賽得佳作英文是 honorable mention。至於首獎英文則是 first prize。prize 這個字本身是獎品的意思，在抽獎時得獎，或是玩遊戲得獎，都用 prize。

award 則是用在經由某些人的評定所給予的獎賞。這個獎賞不一定是獎狀、獎品或名次，主要是評審給予的一種肯定。

place 名次

▶ take first place 得到第一名

That painting took first in the contest.
（那張油畫在比賽中得到第一名。）

She was upset that she only took third.
（她很不高興只得到第三名。）

▶ get (first) place 得到（第一）名

Who got first place?
（第一名是誰？）

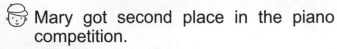

Mary got second place in the piano competition.
（瑪麗在鋼琴比賽中得第二名。）

▶ win (first) place 得（第一）名

Who won first place in that Olympic event?
（在奧林匹克的項目中誰得第一名？）

😊 He was disappointed that he won third place instead of first.
（他對於只得第三名，沒拿到第一名很失望。）

prize 獎品

😊 Did you win a prize at the carnival?
（在園遊會中，你有沒有贏得什麼獎品？）

😊 I won a prize at the fair.
（我在商展中贏到一個獎品。）

😊 I won first prize in the Science Fair.
（在科學展中我得到首獎。）

award 獎賞

😊 You should get an award for this story.
（你這個故事應該得獎。）

😊 Mary received an award for her song.
（瑪麗的歌曲得獎了。）

單字片語

○ award [ə'wɔrd] 獎賞

○ prize [praɪz] 獎品

○ carnival ['kɑrnəvl̩] 園遊會；嘉年華會

○ place [ples] 名次

22 grade school/ elementary school

grade school 和 elementary school 都是小學

對話一

 I remember this from grade school.

（這個我從小學就記得了。）

 Wow, I didn't know it went back that far.

（哇，我不知道它還遠溯到那麼早。）

對話二

 Do you remember when we were in grade school?

（你還記得我們小學時候嗎？）

 Barely. Do you?

（不太記得了，你呢？）

 I remember my teachers asking "What do you want to be when you grow up?".

（我還記得老師問我們說：「你們長大後想做什麼？」）

小秘訣

　英文同一個意思常常會有好幾種不同的説法，例如「小學」，我們學的明明是 elementary school。但在看英文書時，又看到

64

grade school，按照字裏行間的意思，說的明明就是小學，為何不用
elementary school 呢？沒辦法，grade school 也是指小學，這要看
作者喜歡哪個字，二者都可以。

elementary school: 小學

I have known him since elementary school.
（我從小學時就認識他了。）

I don't remember much from my grade
school years.
（我不太記得小學時候的事了。）

▶ grade-school student 小學生

 單字片語

- ○ elementary [ˌɛləˈmɛntərɪ] 基本的

- ○ barely [ˈbɛrlɪ] 勉強地；僅有地

23 secondary school/high school

初中除了可用 secondary school 以外，還有好幾個用法

MP3 24

Where did you go to high school?
（你上哪一所高中？）

I went to Thomas High School.
（我上湯姆斯高中。）

secondary school 初中

Which secondary school did you attend?
（你上哪一所初中？）

▶ junior high school 初中

He was a friend of mine back in junior high.
（他是我初中時的朋友。）

Where did you go to junior high?
（你上哪一所初中？）

▶ middle school 初中

Did you attend band in middle high?
（你初中時有參加樂隊嗎？）

I was a cheerleader in middle school.

（我初中時是啦啦隊。）

high school 高中

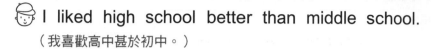

I liked high school better than middle school.

（我喜歡高中甚於初中。）

Our 15th high school reunion is next week.

（我們第 15 屆高中同學會是在下星期。）

▶ senior high 高中

I was in math team when I was in senior high.

（我高中時是數學隊的。）

 單字片語

- ✪ secondary [ˈsɛkəndˌɛrɪ] 中等的

- ✪ band [bænd] 樂隊

- ✪ cheerleader [ˈtʃirˌlidə] 啦啦隊

24 multiple choice questions

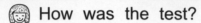

multiple choice questions 到底只有一個答案，還是有 **MP3 25** 多答案？

對話一

 How was the test?

（你考得怎麼樣？）

It was easy. They were all multiple choice questions.

（這次考試很簡單，都是選擇題。）

That should be hard.

（那應該很難。）

Each question could have had several answers.

（每題可能有好幾個答案。）

No. Each question has only one answer in the multiple choice questions.

（不，選擇題每題只有一個答案。）

對話二

 Was the test multiple choice or fill in the blank?

（這次考試是選擇題還是填充題？）

It was both.

（兩項都有。）

來美國唸書的留學生，每個人都一定遇到過 multiple choice questions，到底只要選一個答案，還是會有好幾個答案？依照字面意思來看，台灣來的留學生都認為應該是有好幾個答案，但是美國人的思想很單純，multiple choice 是從好幾個答案當中選一個，就這麼簡單。那麼台灣的多重選擇題英文該如何說呢？那應該是 multiple answer questions。

multiple choice questions 選擇題

My teacher gave us the hardest multiple choice questions.
（我的老師給我們一次最難的選擇題測驗。）

When in doubt, I always choose "C" on multiple choice tests.
（當我不知道答案時，我總是選 "C"。）

What did you put for the first multiple choice question?
（你選擇題第一題選什麼？）

▶ 互相對答案

What did you get on the second question?
（你第二題答什麼？）

I answered "All of the above".
（我答以上皆是。）

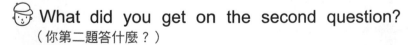

I hope I picked the right answer.
（我希望我選對答案。）

Was "A" the correct answer?
（"A" 是正確答案嗎？）

▶ true/false questions 是非題

Do you prefer True/False questions or multiple choice questions?
（你比較喜歡是非題，還是選擇題？）

multiple answer questions 多重選擇題

That question had multiple answers.
（那道問題有好幾個答案。）

單字片語

- multiple [ˈmʌltəpl̩] 多樣的
- blank [blæŋk] 空白
- fill in 填入；填寫

25 pot quiz/test/exam

老師說要 pop quiz，你還不知道緊張嗎？

MP3 26

對話一

Put your books away. We are having a pop quiz.

（把書本收起來，我們來一次臨時考。）

Oh, no. I didn't study at all.

（噢，不。我都沒唸呢。）

對話二

Are you going to study for the final in History?

（你要準備歷史的期末考嗎？）

Yes. Are you?

（要啊，你呢？）

Yes. Do you want to study together?

（要，你要不要一起唸？）

Yes, I need all the help I can get on this test.

（好啊，只要對這次考試有幫助的我都需要。）

71

小秘訣

留學生在美國常出的另一個洋相，就是當老師宣布 pop quiz，美國同學一面收書本一面唉聲嘆氣。只有你自己一個人「處變不驚」，搞不清楚狀況。弄了半天，才知道老師要來個臨時考了。

examination 是考試的全名，一般人都不喜歡說這個字，而簡單的說 exam。期末考應該是 final examination，一般都簡稱 final exam，或是更簡單地說 final 就行了。

說到考試，用 exam 或 test 都可以。

pop quiz 臨時考

 I hate pop quizzes.
（我討厭臨時考。）

examination 考試

▶ exam 考試

 I have an exam in French tomorrow.
（我明天要考法文。）

▶ mid-term 期中考

 When is our mid-term in this class?
（這門課的期中考是什麼時候？）

 What did you make on the mid-term?

72

（你期中考考幾分？）

Will we have a mid-term in English?
（我們的英文課有期中考嗎？）

▶ final (exam) 期末考

If I make an "A" on this paper, I don't have to take the final.
（如果我的報告成績是 "A"，我就不用考期末考。）

Are you exempt from taking the final exam?
（你可以不需要考期末考嗎？）

▶ test 考試

How did you do on the test?
（你考得如何？）

Do you think the test will be difficult?
（你認為這次考試會很難嗎？）

I made a "B" on the last test.
（上一次的考試我得了 "B"。）

單字片語

○ quiz [kwɪz] 小考

○ exempt [ɪgˊzɛmpt] 免除（義務）

社會新鮮人找工作時，雇主要看的是你的 transcript，而不是 report card

MP3 27

對話一

When will you get your report card?
（你何時會收到成績單？）

Next week, sometime.
（下星期，哪一天都可能。）

How do you think you did this semester?
（你認為你這學期讀得怎麼樣？）

I did okay.
（還好。）

對話二

I need a copy of my transcripts sent to Georgetown University.
（我需要你們寄一份我的成績單到喬治頓大學。）

Just fill out this form and we'll take care of it.
（只要把這張表格填好，我們就會幫你寄。）

　　transcript 和 report card 中文都翻作成績單，但這兩個字卻不是可以混用的。transcript 是指高中或大學的總成績單。你若要申請進入大學，或是要找工作，對方要的是你高中或大學的 transcript，而不是要你的 report card。但是，每次月考完或是每學期結束時，學校寄給家長的則是 report card 而非 transcript。

transcript 成績單（高中或大學時的總成績單）

How much does it cost to get a copy of my transcript?

（申請一份成績單要多少錢？）

You cannot be admitted to college unless they have a copy of your transcript.

（除非你寄成績單給大學，否則你不能去唸。）

I think there is an error on my transcript.

（我認為我的成績單有錯誤。）

I sent you a copy of my transcript.

（我寄了一份成績單給你。）

report card 成績單（每次月考或是每學期的成績單）

My report card was very good this time.

（我這次的成績很好。）

Don't forget to have your parents sign your report card.

（別忘了讓你父母在成績單上簽名。）

Let me see your report card.

（讓我看看你的成績單。）

I got a B on my report card.

（這次的成績單上我有一科 B。）

 單字片語

- ✪ transcript [ˈtrænˌskrɪpt] 成績單

- ✪ semester [səˈmɛstɚ] 學期

- ✪ sign [saɪn] 簽名

- ✪ admit [ədˈmɪt] 許可（入學）

27 major/take

修課的動詞是 take

MP3
28

對話一

What is your major?

（你是哪一系？）

I am a Math major.

（我是數學系的。）

對話二

Do you have to take many science classes?

（你需要修很多科學課嗎？）

No, I only have to take two to graduate.

（不，我只要修兩門就可以畢業。）

You're lucky. I have to take 4 science classes in my major.

（你真幸運，我們這系要修 4 門科學課。）

Good luck.

（祝你好運。）

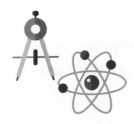

當你想用英文問對方在唸哪一系時,不要問你在哪一個 department(系),而是問 What is your major?

major 主修

What is your major?
(你在哪一系?)

I am majoring in Chemical Engineering.
(我是化學系的。)

I am thinking about changing my major.
(我想轉系。)

▶ minor 副修

I am going to minor in Philosophy.
(我要副修哲學。)

▶ course 課程

Have you had any interesting courses?
(你有沒有上到什麼有趣的課?)

I am not happy with the courses they are offering in my major.
(我對我們系裏開的課很不滿意。)

take 修（課）

 I need to take an English class this semester.

（我這學期要修一門英文。）

I will not take another class from that professor.

（我不會再修那位教授的課了。）

單字片語

○ major ['medʒɚ] 主修

○ professor [prə'fɛsɚ] 教授

28 co-ed / girls' school / boys' school

co-ed 是男女合校

MP3 29

對話一

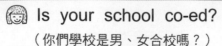 Is your school co-ed?
（你們學校是男、女合校嗎？）

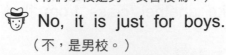 No, it is just for boys.
（不，是男校。）

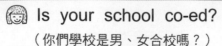 That's too bad.
（那真不好。）

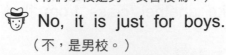 Yes, but girls can visit.
（是的，但女生可以來拜訪。）

對話二

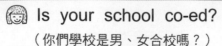 I want to go to a girls' school.
（我要去上女校。）

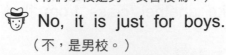 No, you should go to a co-ed school.
（不，你應該去上男女合校。）

小秘訣

co-ed 是 co-education 的簡寫，是指男、女同在一個學術機構受教育。co-ed 不僅可以指學校，也可以用來說宿舍，例如：co-ed dorm 男、女生都收的宿舍；男、女合班也是 co-ed。

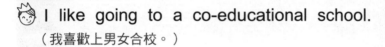
co-ed 男、女合校

I like going to a co-educational school.

（我喜歡上男女合校。）

I like living in co-ed dorms with boys and girls.

（我喜歡住男、女生都有的宿舍。）

▶ girls' school 女校

There are no boys allowed in the girls' school.

（女校不收男生。）

▶ boys' school 男校

Girls are only allowed to visit at certain times in the boys' school.

（男校只允許女生在固定的時間內去拜訪。）

 單字片語

- ✪ visit ['vɪzɪt] 訪問
- ✪ dorm ['dɔrm] 宿舍

對話一

Where are you going?

（你要去哪裏？）

To orientation.

（去新生訓練。）

Me, too.

（我也是。）

Great, come with me.

（那好，跟我一起來。）

對話二

I'm glad we'll have a chance to become acquainted with the school before classes start.

（我很高興在開學前有機會熟悉一下學校。）

Yes, orientation is great.

（是的，新生訓練真好。）

Are you going to the freshman party?

（你要去迎新會嗎？）

Sure, that would be fun.
（當然，那一定很好玩。）

orientation 新生訓練

 I met the President of the university at orientation.
（我在新生訓練時遇到大學的校長。）

 We played fun games at orientation.
（新生訓練時我們玩一些有趣的遊戲。）

 They told us about the school's programs at orientation.
（新生訓練時，他們告訴我們有關學校的課程。）

I met my teachers at orientation.

（我在新生訓練時遇見我的老師。）

freshman party 迎新會

The programs at the freshman party were interesting.

（迎新會上的節目很有趣。）

▶ freshman dance 迎新舞會

I had a good time at the freshman dance.

（迎新舞會上我玩得很愉快。）

單字片語

- ✪ acquaint [ə'kwent] +with 把～告知（某人）；使熟識～（某人）

- ✪ orientation [ˌorɪɛn'teʃən] 新生訓練

30 diploma/certificate

畢業證書是 diploma，而 certificate 的用途更廣泛

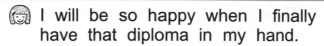

MP3
31

對話

 I will be so happy when I finally have that diploma in my hand.

（當我終於拿到畢業證書時，我會很高興。）

I know what you mean.

（我瞭解你的意思。）

小秘訣

　　完成學業從學校畢業時，拿到的證書叫 diploma。至於其他的證明書，則用 certificate。certificate 可用來指很多用途的證明書，例如：修完一種課程的證書 certificate of completion for that course，或 certificate of accomplishment（結業證書），頒給成績優異的證明書 certificate for outstanding work（獎狀）。其他如結婚證書、出生證明等，都是拿到一張 certificate。

diploma 畢業證書

 I can't wait to get my diploma.

（我等不及拿到我的畢業證書。）

I am going to frame my diploma and put it in my office.

（我要把畢業證書框起來，掛在辦公室。）

Look at all of his diplomas on the wall.

（看看他牆上掛的那些畢業證書。）

The President handed me the diploma as I crossed the stage.

（當我走過講台時，校長把畢業證書遞給我。）

Where are you going to hang your diploma?

（你要把畢業證書掛在哪裏？）

certificate 證明書

Did you get a certificate of completion for that course?

（你有沒有收到那門課的結業證書？）

My school sent me a certificate for outstanding work.

（我的學校寄給我一張獎狀。）

They are mailing me a certificate of accomplishment.

（他們會寄給我一張結業證書。）

I have a certificate of enrollment for this class.

（我有這門課的入學證書。）

- ✪ diploma [dɪ'plomə] 畢業證書

- ✪ certificate [sə'tɪfəkət] 證明書

- ✪ birth certificate 出生證明書

- ✪ marriage certificate 結婚證明書

- ✪ outstanding [ˌaʊt'stændɪŋ] 傑出的

- ✪ accomplishment [ə'kɑmplɪʃmənt] 完成

- ✪ frame [frem] 裝框

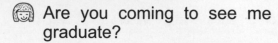

對話一

 Are you coming to see me graduate?

（你要來看我畢業嗎？）

I would not miss your commencement for the world.

（無論如何我都不會錯過你的畢業典禮。）

對話二

 I'm really looking forward to getting that diploma.

（我真的好期待拿到那張畢業證書。）

Well, you earned it.

（那是你努力得來的。）

對話三

 What time is your graduation ceremony?

（你的畢業典禮是幾點？）

It is at 1:00.

（1 點。）

commencement 是畢業典禮的英文字,但是説 graduation ceremony 也可以。

commencement 畢業典禮

That was a lovely commencement.
（那是一場極佳的畢業典禮。）

Will you participate in commencement?
（你會參加畢業典禮嗎？）

You will receive your diploma at commencement.
（畢業典禮時你會接到畢業證書。）

I hope the commencement exercises don't take too long.
（我希望畢業典禮的過程別太久。）

graduation ceremony 畢業典禮

I enjoyed the graduation ceremony.
（我喜歡畢業典禮。）

When is your graduation ceremony?
（你的畢業典禮是幾點？）

▶ graduation invitation 畢業典禮邀請函

Did you receive my graduation invitation?
（你有沒有收到我的畢業典禮邀請函？）

▶ graduate 畢業

I'm sorry I was not there to see you graduate.
（很抱歉我沒去看你畢業典禮。）

Has he graduated yet?
（他畢業了沒？）

How long ago did you graduate?
（你多久前畢業的？）

 單字片語

- ✪ commencement [kə'mɛnsmənt] 畢業典禮

- ✪ graduate ['grædʒʊ,et] v. 畢業

- ✪ graduation [,grædʒʊ'eʃən]　n. 畢業

- ✪ ceremony ['sɛrə,monɪ] 儀式

- ✪ participate [pɑr'tɪsə,pet]　參加

alumnus/alumni association/alma mater

校友、母校這些奇怪的英文字是源自於拉丁文

MP3 33

對話一

 Did you attend Yale?

（你上耶魯大學嗎？）

 Yes, I am an alumnus of Yale.

（是的，我是耶魯的校友。）

 Me too.

（我也是。）

Nice to meet you.

（你好。）

對話二

 I'm going to join the Alumni association.

（我要參加校友會。）

 What is that?

（那是什麼？）

It's a group of people who have graduated from here who are still active with the school.

（那是一群從這學校畢業，仍熱中於校務的人。）

 What do you do?

（你們做什麼事？）

91

We help the school raise money to give it better programs.

（我們幫忙學校募捐，讓學校有更好的課程。）

Why?

（為什麼？）

Because we are proud of our alma mater.

（因為我們以母校為榮。）

小秘訣

校友這個字的英文字單數是 alumnus；複數是 alumni，而校友會是由許多校友組成，所以要用複數 alumni association。

alumnus 校友（複數形是 alumni）

He is a distinguished alumnus.
（他是位傑出校友。）

He is a fellow alumnus of this college.
（他是這個學校的校友。）

▶ graduate 畢業生

Are you a graduate of this school?
（你是這個學校的畢業生嗎？）

alumni association 校友會

I am President of my alumni association.
（我是我們校友會的會長。）

Are you a member of the alumni association?
（你是校友會的會員嗎？）

I am not an active member of the alumni association.
（我並不是校友會裏活躍的會員。）

alma mater: 母校

Where is your alma mater?
（你的母校在哪裏？）

Our alma mater is having a reunion.
（我的母校將有個同學會。）

I give a lot of money to my alma mater.
（我捐很多錢給母校。）

單字片語

- alumnus [ə'lʌmnəs] 校友
- alumni [ə'lʌmnaɪ] 校友（複數形）
- association [ə,sosɪ'eʃən] 協會
- alma mater ['ælmə 'metɚ] 母校

93

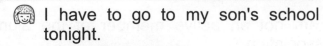

33 PTA/teacher conference

母姐會是 teacher conference，或是 PTA meeting；
家長會是 PTA

MP3 34

對話一

 I have to go to my son's school tonight.

（我今晚要去我兒子的學校。）

 For PTA?

（參加家長會嗎？）

 No, I have to have a conference with his teacher.

（不是，我要去跟他的老師談話。）

 I hope all goes well.

（我希望一切都很順利。）

對話二

 I am a member of the Parent/ Teacher Association.

（我是家長會的會員。）

 Yes, I am also a member of the PTA.

（我也是家長會的會員。）

小秘訣

　　PTA 是 Parent/Teacher Association 的簡寫。台灣的母姊會英文可說成 PTA meeting，因為 PTA meeting 就是學校報告一些校務，然後家長可以和老師座談。母姊會也可以說成 teacher conference，不過 teacher conference 大多是家長一對一與老師對談。

PTA 家長會

Do you belong to the PTA at your children's school?

（你加入了你小孩學校的家長會嗎？）

We would like you to join the PTA.

（我們想要你加入家長會。）

My parents are in the PTA.

（我的父母在家長會。）

conference 座談會

I would like to have a conference with your teacher.

（我想要跟你的老師談話。）

I'm going to a teacher conference this afternoon.

（今天下午我要去跟老師談話。）

How long has it been since your last teacher conference?

（離你上次和老師談話有多久了？）

▶ talk to the teacher 和老師談話

I would like to talk to your teacher.

（我想要和你的老師談話。）

When would you like to schedule a time to meet?

（你想要安排在什麼時候見面？）

My teacher would like to talk to you tomorrow.

（我們老師明天要跟你談話。）

○ conference ['kɑnfərəns] 會議；座談會

classmate / someone in my class

說到同學，兩者都可以用

MP3 35

對話一

Who is that?

（那是誰？）

He is a classmate of mine.

（他是我的同學。）

Does he have a girlfriend?

（他有女朋友嗎？）

I don't know. I'll ask him during class.

（我不知道，我上課時會問他。）

對話二

That guy has been in the same classes with me since junior high.

（那傢伙從初中時就一直跟我同班。）

Wow. That's a long time.

（哇，那可真久。）

小秘訣

　說到同學，英文有一個單字就是 classmate，若不記這個單字的話，也可以說 someone in my class。如果要強調「同班上課」，那就是 be in the same class。

classmate 同學

I'll get the notes from a classmate.
（我會從同學處拿筆記。）

This book belongs to my classmate.
（這本書是我同學的。）

I don't know any of my classmates.
（我不認識班上的任何人。）

▶ in the same class 同班

Aren't you in the same class as me?
（你不是跟我同班嗎？）

We took French together in high school.
（我們高中時一起修法文。）

We have been in the same classes since 6th grade.
（我們從 6 年級起就一直同班。）

▶ someone in my class 我的同學

I'll get the notes from someone in my class.
（我會從我同學那裏拿筆記。）

單字片語

- classmate ['klæs,met] 同學

- note [not] 筆記

98

35 flunk/pass/fail

考試不及格是 fail，當掉是 flunk

MP3
36

對話一

Did you pass the test?
（你考試及格了嗎？）

Yes, I scored 90 points out of 100.
（是的，我考了 90 分。）

Really? I got a 92.
（真的？我考了 92 分）

Way to go.
（真不錯。）

對話二

Well, I flunked my algebra test.
（我的代數當掉了。）

Yes, I failed it, too.
（我也是考不及格。）

小秘訣

　考試考不及格，正式的英語說法是 fail。台灣的學生喜歡說某科被當，英語可以說 flunk。

考試時滿分不一定是 100 分，為了使意思更清楚，正式一點的說法是 scored 90 points out of 100.（滿分是 100 分我考了 90 分）。如果大家都知道總分是 100 分時，可以簡單說 My English score was 90. 或是 I got a 90 on English test.（我英文考了 90 分）。

pass 考及格

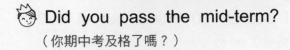 Did you pass the mid-term?
（你期中考及格了嗎？）

I passed this one with flying colors.
（這次考試我輕輕鬆鬆就及格了。）

I hope I at least passed.
（我希望我至少能及格。）

I didn't pass the test.
（我沒有及格。）

flunk 當掉（指考試的成績）

I'm sure I flunked that one.
（那科我確實是當掉了。）

I flunked this one bad.
（我這科當得好慘。）

▶ fail 考不及格

I'm afraid I failed that test.
（我恐怕那次考試考不及格。）

You're going to flunk if you don't study.
（如果你不讀書你會被當。）

At least I didn't fail.
（至少我沒有考不及格。）

▶ okay 還好

Did you do okay on the test?
（你考得還好嗎？）

 單字片語

○ with flying colors 做得又好又輕鬆

○ flunk [flʌŋk] 當掉

36 no school/have school

不用上學的道地英語是 There is no school.

對話一

Do you have school next week?

（你下星期要上學嗎？）

No, it's Spring Break.

（不用，放春假了。）

It's my Spring Break, too.

（我也是放春假。）

Let's go to the beach.

（我們到海邊去玩。）

對話二

A good news. Do you want to know about it?

（好消息，你要不要聽？）

What have you heard?

（你聽到什麼消息？）

The typhoon is coming tomorrow. There will be no school.

（颱風明天要來了，不用上學。）

對話三

The final exam is two weeks from now.

（離期末考還有兩個星期。）

We're not having class next week.

（我們下星期不上課。）

 If we have problems, how do we contact you?

（如果我們有問題，如何聯絡你？）

 I'll be in my office every morning.

（我每天早上都會在辦公室。）

（註：這段對話是大學教授與學生的對話。A 是教授，B 是學生。）

小秘訣

　　have school 是指學校沒停課要上學。但在大學裡並不是每一堂都有課，所以即使學校沒停課，大學生在一天內也只有幾節課要上，就要說 have class。

　　為了某些原因不上課，如：颱風放假、學校停課等，英語說法是 There is no school.。

no school 不用上學

 There is no school next Friday.
（下星期五不用上學。）

 I hope there is no school today.
（我希望今天不用上學。）

Next Tuesday is a holiday, so there will be no school.
（下星期二放假，所以不用上學。）

have school 要上學

Are we having school today?
（我們今天要上學嗎？）

▶ have class 要上課（大半是講大學生）

Do you have class this afternoon?
（你今天下午有課嗎？）

We're not having class next week.
（我們下星期沒課。）

▶ a day off from school 放假一天；請假一天

I hope we get a snow day off from school.
（我希望能因下雪放假一天。）

I would like the day off from school.
（我想請假一天。）

 單字片語

- ✪ beach [bitʃ] 海濱

- ✪ contact ['kɑntækt] 聯絡

37 field day/sports day

運動會的英語是 field day 或 sports day

MP3
38

對話

Tomorrow is field day.
（明天是運動會。）

Do I need to bring anything?
（我需要帶什麼東西嗎？）

No, just wear comfortable clothes.
（不，只要穿得舒服一點。）

I will.
（我會的。）

小秘訣

運動會在美國就叫 field day 或 sports day，你若按中文字面意思去直譯，美國人會聽不懂。

field day 運動會

I like to participate in field day.
（我喜歡參加運動會。）

I won the potato sack race at field day.

（運動會時我贏了沙袋競走。）

I liked the games we played at field day.

（我喜歡我們在運動會時的比賽。）

When are we having another field day?

（我們何時才會有運動會？）

sports day 運動會

I won first prize at sports day.

（我運動會時得到第一名。）

 單字片語

- ⊙ comfortable [ˈkʌmfɚˌtəbl] 舒服的
- ⊙ participate [pɑrˈtɪsəˌpet] 參加
- ⊙ race [res] 賽跑

38 golf course / tennis court

高爾夫球場，網球場

對話一

 I saw you out on the tennis courts today.

（今天我在網球場看到你。）

 What time?

（什麼時候？）

 Around noon.

（大概在中午。）

 Yes, that was me.

（是的，那是我。）

對話二

 I'm going to the driving range.

（我要去高爾夫球練習場。）

 Go without me. I don't like golf.

（你自己去就好，我不喜歡打高爾夫。）

小秘訣

course 和 court 都是指一塊做為運動或比賽的場地，但說到高

爾夫球場，習慣上都是說 golf course；而籃球場或網球場則用 basketabll court 和 tennis court。

注意：高爾夫球練習場英文不是 golf practice course，它有一個特定的名稱叫 driving range。

足球場不叫 course，也不叫 court。而叫 football field。

golf course 高爾夫球場

Which course do you prefer to play golf at?
（你比較喜歡在哪一個高爾夫球場打球？）

I don't like that course.
（我不喜歡那個球場。）

We play golf on the golf course next to the Evergreen park.
（我們在長春公園旁的高爾夫球場打球。）

▶ driving range 高爾夫球練習場

I like the driving range on First Street.
（我喜歡第一街上的高爾夫球練習場。）

I've lost a lot of balls on that driving range.
（我在那個高爾夫球練習場丟掉好多球。）

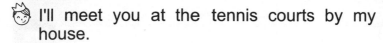 I'll meet you at the tennis courts by my house.

（我會在我家旁邊的網球場見你。）

Where do you play tennis?

（你在哪裏打網球？）

The courts at the high school are the best.

（那所高中的球場是最好的。）

 單字片語

- ⊙ course [kors]（球）場
- ⊙ court [kort]（球）場
- ⊙ range [rendʒ] 區
- ⊙ next to ～ 在～之旁

39 field trip/tour

field trip 是有教育意義的旅行；tour 有時也具有教育意義，但也可以只是普通旅行

MP3 40

對話一

I can't wait to go on the field trip.
（我等不及去遠足。）

Where are you going?
（你們要去哪裏？）

To the planetarium.
（去天文台。）

Wow, can I go?
（哇，我可以去嗎？）

對話二

Our band is going on a tour.
（我們樂團要去旅行。）

That sounds like fun.
（聽起來很棒。）

小秘訣

　　遠足的英文該怎麼説呢？這要依遠足的性質來看了。因為 field trip 是指由學校帶隊，去動物園、科學館、博物館等地方參觀，也就是去實地參觀課堂上學到的東西。若該次遠足不是校外教學，只是到野外去踏青，那就叫 go on a picnic。

　　tour 則是出去旅行，不是校外教學，也不是出去踏青。tour 當動詞是「參觀」的意思。

field trip 遠足;（學生的）實地考察旅行

Do I need to bring my lunch for the field trip?
（這次遠足需要帶中飯嗎？）

We are having a field trip to the farm next week.
（我們下星期要到農場去遠足。）

tour 旅行;觀光

Where is your choir going on a tour?
（你們合唱團要去哪裏旅行？）

We are going to tour the museum.
（我們要去參觀博物館。）

picnic 野餐

What should I bring to the picnic?
（我該帶什麼去野餐？）

My Spanish class is going on a picnic next week.
（我們西班牙文課下星期要去野餐。）

 單字片語

- ☺ tour [tʊr] 旅行
- ☺ field [fild]（學習的）領域
- ☺ farm [fɑrm] 農場

40 finish/be done

I'm done. 不是說我完蛋了，而是說事情做完了

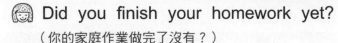

MP3 41

對話一

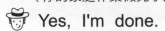 Did you finish your homework yet?

（你的家庭作業做完了沒有？）

Yes, I'm done.

（是的，做完了。）

對話二

Are you through with your assignment yet?

（你的作業做完了沒？）

Not yet. But I'm almost done.

（還沒，但是快做完了。）

小秘訣

事情做完了的英文是 finish 或 be through，但口語上 I'm done.（我做完了）也是常見的說法。雖然 I'm done. 這種說法，某些保守的美國人不能接受，他們認為聽起來有一種「我完蛋了」的味道。但既然大部分美國人都這樣說，我們也最好跟著學。

be done 做完了

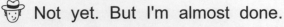 I'm done with my part of the chores.

（我做完了我該做的雜務。）

When you're done, let me know.
（當你做完時，讓我知道。）

finish 做完

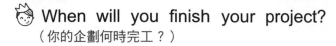 When will you finish your project?
（你的企劃何時完工？）

 When you're finished washing the dishes, go clean up your room.
（你把碗洗完後，去把房間整理乾淨。）

▶ 把（食物）吃完

 Finish your green beans.
（把你的綠豆吃完。）

be through 做完

Are you through with the paper yet?
（你的報告做完了沒？）

單字片語

- ☉ finish ['fɪnɪʃ] 做完
- ☉ assignment [ə'saɪnmənt] 指定作業
- ☉ homework ['hom,wɝk] 家庭作業
- ☉ chore [tʃor] 雜務
- ☉ paper ['pepɚ] 報告

41 be over/end

節目、事情結束了

MP3
42

對話

 When will that TV show be over?
（那個電視節目何時結束？）

It ends at 9:00.
（9 點。）

小秘訣

　　說某個節目、某件事情結束用動詞 **end**。若要用 **over** 這個字，前面要加個 **be** 動詞 **be over**。

end 結束

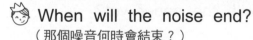

When will the noise end?
（那個噪音何時會結束？）

I'm going to put an end to this.
（我要把這件事結束掉。）

▶ be over 結束

I'll be glad when this day is over.
（我很高興今天過去了。）

 單字片語

○ noise [nɔɪz] 噪音

114

42 fun/funny

某人 feel funny 可不是一件 fun 的事

MP3
43

對話一

 I like Mary.
（我喜歡瑪麗。）

Yes, she is a fun person.
（是的，她是一個很有趣的人。）

對話二

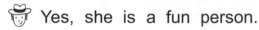 What's wrong with you?
（你怎麼啦？）

I just feel a little funny.
（我只是覺得不太對勁。）

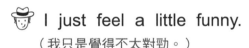 Do you think you are coming down
with something?
（你想你是不是病了？）

No, I'm just tired.
（不，我只是很累而已。）

小秘訣

　　funny 是好笑的意思。若説某人很 funny，是説那個人喜歡搞笑，或是説那個人很可笑。但是 fun 是指樂趣、有趣，若説某人是 a fun person，是指那個人興趣廣泛，説話風趣，跟他在一起不覺得無聊。

　　funny 也可以説某個人或某件東西不對。例如：I'm feeling a little funny.（我覺得不太對勁，不太舒服）。所以有人覺得 funny 時，可不是一件 fun 的事。

funny 好笑的

 I just heard the funniest joke.
（我剛聽到最好笑的笑話。）

▶ funny guy 可笑的傢伙

 Tommy is such a funny guy.
（湯米是這樣一個可笑的傢伙。）

▶ feel funny 覺得不舒服

 I'm feeling a little funny.
（我覺得不太舒服。）

fun 有趣；好玩

 I've heard the dance was a lot of fun.
（我聽説那次舞會很好玩。）

We always have fun together.

（我們在一起總是玩得很愉快。）

▶ 有趣的

Mr. Lin is such a fun person.

（林先生是這樣一個有趣的人。）

單字片語

- come down with 〜 生〜病
- come down with a cold 感冒了
- joke [dʒok] 笑話

43 close call / emergency

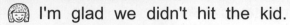

emergency 是必須馬上處理的緊急事件；close call
只是虛驚一場

**MP3
44**

對話一

 I'm glad we didn't hit the kid.

（我很高興我們沒撞到那個小孩。）

That was a close call.

（真是千鈞一髮。）

 I never expected someone would come out all of a sudden.

（我沒想到會有人突然出來。）

I hope the kid would learn the lesson.

（我希望那小孩能學到教訓。）

對話二

 Operator, how can I connect you?

（這裏是接線生，要接哪裏？）

This is an emergency. Give me the police.

（是緊急狀況。接警察局。）

小秘訣

　　emergency 是緊急事件，指已經發生的意外。a close call 是千鈞
一髮，指意外差一點就發生，幸好沒發生。

a close call 千鈞一髮

That was a close call. We almost had an accident.
（剛剛真是千鈞一髮，我們差點就出車禍了。）

emergency 緊急狀況；緊急事件

This is an emergency.
（這是緊急事件。）

Who should we notify in the case of an emergency?
（一旦有緊急事件，我們該通知誰？）

Dial 911 for emergency.
（有緊急事件時撥 911。）

 單字片語

- ❂ emergency [ɪˈmɝdʒənsɪ] 緊急事件
- ❂ notify [ˈnotəˌfaɪ] 通知
- ❂ dial [ˈdaɪəl] 撥（電話）
- ❂ all of a sudden 突然地
- ❂ learn the lesson 學到教訓
- ❂ accident [ˈæksədənt] 意外事件

44 keep / raise / grow

在家裡養寵物和在外面養動物的「養」字不一樣

MP3
45

Mom, there is a kitten following me home.

（媽，有一隻小貓跟著我回家。）

Can I keep it?

（我可不可以養它？）

I'm afraid not, honey. We can't keep a pet in the apartment.

（恐怕不行。在公寓裏不可以養寵物的。）

What do you raise on your farm?

（你農場上養什麼動物？）

We raise cattle.

（我們養牛。）

Do you grow anything?

（你有沒有種什麼？）

Yes, we grow corn and tomatoes.

（有，我們種玉米和馬鈴薯。）

養動物、小孩動詞用 raise，但是在家裏面養寵物卻用 keep。至於種植物動詞用 grow。

grow 種（植物）；（植物）生長；留（指甲）

Do you know how to grow lettuce?
（你知道如何種生菜嗎？）

I can't believe how much this plant has grown.
（我真不敢相信這植物長得這麼多。）

I cannot grow fingernails.
（我不能留指甲。）

keep 養（寵物）

How many rabbits do you keep?
（你養了幾隻兔子？）

The landlord wouldn't let us keep a pet.
（房東不准我們養寵物。）

raise 養（動物）；扶養小孩

Raising children is hard work.
（養小孩是很辛苦的工作。）

I've raised this cow since she was a calf.
（這隻牛是我從小把它養大的。）

Are you any good at raising sheep?
（你會牧羊嗎？）

 單字片語

- ✪ raise [rez] 飼養
- ✪ pet [pɛt] 寵物
- ✪ cattle [ˈkætl̩] 牛
- ✪ landlord [ˈlændˌlɔrd] 房東
- ✪ calf [kæf] 小牛
- ✪ cow [kaʊ] 母牛

45 send / deliver

你自己不親自 deliver 時，就是要用 send

MP3 46

對話一

 I would like to send a dozen roses to my wife.

（我要送一打玫瑰花給我太太。）

 What address would you like them sent to?

（你要花送到哪裏？）

對話二

 The newsboy didn't deliver papers today.

（報童今天沒送報來。）

 You should call before 10 o'clock to have one delivered.

（那你要在早上 10 點以前打電話去要他們送一份來。）

小秘訣

　　send 和 deliver 中文都翻成「送」的意思，實際上這兩個字的用法不一樣。當報童送報來時要用 deliver；當你到花店要送花給某人時要用 send。因為 deliver 是某人親自送某物到某地，例如：報童拿著報紙 deliver 到你家；而 send 是要派人送東西到某地，不是你自己親自去送。所以例句中，你告訴花店店員要 send 玫瑰花給你太太時，是請花店派人送玫瑰花去，不是你自己親自 deliver。

send 送；寄

Did you send her flowers?
（你有送她花嗎？）

I will send your jacket to you.
（我會把你的夾克寄給你。）

▶ send for 派人去請～來

Mary is quite ill. Please send for the doctor.
（瑪麗病得很重，請派人去請醫生來。）

deliver 送

The store will deliver our TV set.
（商店會把我們的電視送來。）

The courier will deliver the package tomorrow.
（信差明天會送包裹。）

 單字片語

- ○ newsboy 報童
- ○ courier [ˈkʊrɪɚ] 信差
- ○ package [ˈpækɪdʒ] 包裹

46 telephone / call

telephone、phone 和 call 的用法都一樣

對話一

 Was that the telephone?

（是電話嗎？）

Yes, it's for you.

（是的，你的電話。）

對話二

I promised her I would call her tonight.

（我答應她今晚會打電話給她。）

But, you just got off the phone 10 minutes ago.

（但是，你10分鐘前才打完電話。）

I know, but I promised I'd phone her.

（我知道，但我答應要打電話給她的。）

Fine, just let me know when you're done.

（好吧，你打完後告訴我一聲。）

　　telephone, phone 和 call 這三個字都可以當動詞，「打電話」的意思；當名詞則指「電話」。三個字的用法都一樣。

phone 打電話；電話

▶ 當動詞

Who was that who phoned?
（打電話的人是誰？）

Should I phone him this late?
（這麼晚了，我可以打電話給他嗎？）

▶ telephone 打電話；電話

I'll try telephoning later.
（等一下再打打看。）

Can you hear the telephone if it rings?
（如果電話鈴響了，你聽得到嗎？）

call 打電話；電話

▶ 當動詞

I'll call you tomorrow.
（我明天打電話給你。）

😊 Did you call him back?
（你回他電話了嗎？）

😄 Who called?
（誰打來的？）

▶ 當名詞

😊 I don't want to miss her call.
（我不想錯過她的電話。）

😄 Did you return her call?
（你回她的電話了嗎？）

▶ call someone up 打電話給某人

😊 I think I'll call her up.
（我想我要打個電話給她。）

 單字片語

- promise [ˈprɑmɪs] 保證

- miss [mɪs] 錯過

- return [rɪˈtɜn] 回（電話）

47 learn / study

learn 是學習隨時隨地都會發生的事；study 則需要特別撥時間去學習

MP3 48

對話一

What did you learn in school today?

（你今天在學校裏學到什麼？）

We studied about Chinese history.

（我們今天唸中國歷史。）

對話二

My math class is so boring.

（數學課好無聊。）

Why?

（為什麼？）

I am not learning anything.

（我什麼也沒學到。）

Maybe you're not trying hard enough.

（或許你不夠認真。）

小秘訣

learn 指學習；學東西。在任何地方、任何情況，甚至於從周圍的人，你都可以 learn something。

study 則是真正把書本翻開，讀書或唸書。

learn 學習

Can you help me learn this?
（你能幫我學這個嗎？）

Are you learning anything from tutorials?
（你從個別指導學到什麼？）

Who says learning isn't fun?
（誰說學習不好玩？）

I learned something interesting today.
（我今天學到一些好玩的事。）

He learned the second verse to the song.
（他學了這首歌的第二段。）

I haven't learned a thing.
（我什麼也沒學到。）

study 讀書；唸書

Shouldn't you be studying?
（你不是應該在唸書嗎？）

I studied for this test all night long.
（我整晚都在唸書。）

單字片語

- history ['hɪstrɪ] 歷史
- boring ['borɪŋ] 很乏味
- tutorial [tu'torɪəl] 個別指導
- verse [vɝs]（一首歌的）段

48 bargain / good deal

bargain 也可以說是一個 good deal

對話

I can't believe you went shopping.
（我真不敢相信你會去買東西。）

But this was on sale.
（但是現在正在打折啊。）

I'll bet it was a real bargain.
（我打賭價錢一定不貴。）

Yes, I got a good deal.
（是的，我買得很便宜。）

小秘訣

打折拍賣的東西並不一定便宜。用好的價錢買到便宜的東西是 bargain，或是 a good deal。

bargain 真正便宜的東西

This shirt was such a bargain.
（這件襯衫真的很便宜。）

130

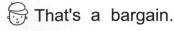 That's a bargain.

（那真的很便宜。）

At ten thousands dollars, this car is a bargain.

（以 1 萬元來說，這車真的是買得便宜。）

a good deal 真正划算的買賣

They had a good price on it.

（他們的價錢很便宜。）

I got a good deal on this.

（這東西買得很划算。）

What a deal!

（價錢真的便宜！）

 單字片語

- ✪ bargain ['bɑrgɪn] 便宜貨

- ✪ deal [dil] 交易

- ✪ go shopping 去買東西；購物

49 sale / on sale / for sale

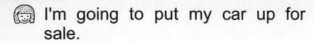

for sale 不是打折拍賣，sale 和 on sale 才是

MP3
50

對話一

 I'm going to put my car up for sale.

（我要賣我的車子。）

I'll buy it.

（我要買。）

對話二

Sogo had a sale yesterday.

（崇光百貨昨天在打折拍賣。）

When will the sale be over?

（拍賣什麼時候結束？）

It's a one-day sale. I believe it's over.

（只拍賣一天，我相信已經結束了。）

Oh, what a shame!

（噢，多可惜。）

Don't feel bad. I didn't see any bargains at all.

（別難過，我沒有看到真正便宜的東西。）

132

小秘訣

　　sale 這個字是 sell 的名詞，本身意思是出售（東西），也可以做打折拍賣用。到底 sale 是指出售還是打折拍賣？你可以從句子的前後文看出來。

　　另外兩個片語 on sale 和 for sale 不能隨便混用：on sale 只用於說東西在打折拍賣，for sale 是說東西要出售，絕沒有拍賣的意思。

　　至於 garage sale 是美國特有的產物，美國人不用的舊東西會清理出來在車庫中拍賣，叫做 garage sale。

sale 打折拍賣

▶ sale 打折拍賣

The department store is having a sale on shoes.
（百貨公司的鞋子正在打折。）

I'm going to the Far-East department store. It's the last day of the sale.
（我要去遠東百貨公司，今天是打折的最後一天。）

You should take advantage of this sale and buy now.
（你應該利用打折的時候買。）

▶ on sale 打折拍賣

I got this blouse on sale.
（我在打折時買了這件上衣。）

I only buy things when they are on sale.
（我只在打折時買東西。）

▶ garage sale 在車庫裏賣舊貨

▶ a clearance sale 清倉大拍賣

for sale 出售

Is this vase for sale?
（這個花瓶要賣嗎？）

John made two hundred dollars on the sale of his computer.
（約翰賣他的電腦賺了二百元。）

（這句話裏的 sale 是出售的意思）

Will you sell this to me for $10?
（這個你可以賣我 10 塊錢嗎？）

 單字片語

○ sale [sel] 出售；打折拍賣

○ department store [dɪ'pɑrtmənt stor] 百貨公司

○ advantage [əd'væntɪdʒ] 利益

○ take advantage of ～ 利用～

○ garage [gə'rɑʒ] 車庫

50 sold out / booked up

booked up 是被預訂一空

對話一

 Do you have any tickets for tonight's performance?

（你有今晚表演的票嗎？）

Mo, I'm sorry we are sold out.

（沒有，很抱歉都賣完了。）

對話二

 I need to get a hotel room for next week.

（我需要為下星期訂一間旅館房間。）

I'm sorry. We're all booked up.

（對不起，我們的房間都被預定光了。）

小秘訣

東西或是票被賣完了用 sold out。被預定光了，要説 booked up。

票都賣完了，你可以説 We're sold out. 或是 They're sold out.。

房間或是座位都被訂光，你可以説 We're all booked up. 或是 They're all booked up.。

sold out 賣光了

Is the concert sold out?
（音樂會的票都賣光了嗎？）

They sold out my favorite candy.
（我最喜歡的糖果都賣光了。）

booked up 預定一空

I couldn't get a room. They were all booked up.
（我訂不到房間，都被訂光了。）

The show is booked solid for three months.
（那項表演三個月的票全都被訂光了。）

Are you all booked up?
（都被訂光了嗎？）

Is everything booked?
（都被訂完了嗎？）

 單字片語

- ticket ['tɪkɪt] 票

- performance [pɚ'fɔrməns] 表演

- concert ['kɑnsɚt] 音樂會

51 cheers / toast / bottomes up

向人敬酒是 toast；cheers 和 bottoms up 是喝酒前說的

對話一

 I'd like to propose a toast to our guest of honor.

（我提議向我們的貴賓敬酒。）

 Cheers.

（大家喝。）

 Bottoms up.

（乾杯。）

對話二

 Let's toast to the birthday girl.

（讓我們向壽星敬酒。）

 To Mary.

（敬瑪麗。）

 Cheers.

（大家喝酒。）

toast 當敬酒的意思，可以做動詞和名詞。當名詞時，通常都用 propose 這個動詞來提議給誰 a toast。

很多人一起喝酒時，通常會一面喝酒一面說乾杯。說大家一起喝，英語是 Cheers.；若說乾杯，英語是 Bottoms up.。

toast 乾杯

The guests proposed toasts to the bride and groom at the wedding party.

（來賓在婚禮上向新郎、新娘敬酒。）

Every one toasted to Mr. Lin on his farewell party.

（在林先生的歡送會上，每個人都向他敬酒。）

▶ 喝酒時

Bottoms up.

（乾杯。）

Cheers.

（大家喝。）

▶ 敬酒時

Here's to our health.

（為我們的健康喝一杯。）

Best wishes.
（最好的祝福。）

 Here's to friends.
（敬我們的朋友。）

 單字片語

- ✪ propose [prə'poz] 提議
- ✪ Toast [tost] 敬酒
- ✪ wedding ['wɛdɪŋ] 婚禮
- ✪ farewell [ˌfɛr'wɛl]　再見
- ✪ bride [braɪd] 新娘
- ✪ groom [grum] 新郎

52 treat / go Dutch

請客、或各付各的說法有很多種，學會了，選適當的來說

對話一

 I'd like to take you out to dinner.

（我想帶你去吃晚飯。）

 Is it your treat?

（你要請客嗎？）

 Of course.

（當然。）

 Great.

（好棒。）

對話二

 Would you bring me the check, please?

（請把帳單給我。）

 Let me have the check. It's my treat.

（帳單給我。我請客。）

 Oh no. Tell you what. Let's go Dutch.

（哦，不。我說我們就各付各的吧。）

 No. I'm paying and that's that.

（不，我付，就這麼辦。）

請客正式的英文單字是 treat。但口語上也有其他的說法,例如用 buy、on 或 pay 等,以下的例句很詳盡,你可以學會如何使用。

至於各付各的可以說 go Dutch。口語一點可以說 Let's each pay for our own way.。

treat 請客

I'd like to treat you to dinner.
(我想請你去吃晚飯。)

I'd like this dinner to be my treat.
(今晚由我請客。)

Drinks will be my treat.
(飲料我來付。)

Is it your treat?
(是你請客嗎?)

Are you treating?
(你要請客嗎?)

▶ buy 請客

Let me buy your lunch.
(讓我請你吃午飯。)

Let me buy you a drink.
(讓我請你喝一杯。)

▶ on 請客

Dinner is on me.
（晚飯由我請客。）

▶ pay 付錢

It's your turn to pay.
（輪到你付錢。）

I'll pay.
（我來付。）

▶ pick up the check 拿帳單

I'll pick up the check.
（帳單我來負責。）

go Dutch 各付各的

Let's go Dutch treat.
（我們就各付各的。）

Let's each pay for our own way.
（讓我們各付各的。）

- treat [trit] 請客

- check [tʃɛk] 帳單

- turn [tɝn] 輪流

53 liquor / drink

平時英語說喝酒都是用 drink，而不說 liquor

MP3 54

對話一

Do you want another drink?

（你要再來一杯嗎？）

Oh, no, thanks. I've enough liquor tonight. I'm getting drunk.

（噢，不要了，我今晚已經喝得夠多，我有點醉了。）

Not you. You really know how to hold your liquor.

（你不會醉的，你的酒量很好的。）

Sorry. I'll pass on this one.

（抱歉，這一輪我不喝了。）

對話二

Can I get you anything to drink?

（你要什麼飲料嗎？）

Coke, please.

（請給我可樂。）

We're going to the bar after work. Would you like to come along?

（下班後我們要去酒吧，你要不要一起來？）

No, thanks.

（不，謝謝。）

Don't you drink?

（你不喝酒嗎？）

When I was in college, I went drinking almost every weekend.

（我大學時，我幾乎每個週末都去喝酒。）

But I can't take alcohol any more.

（但現在不能再喝了。）

小秘訣

　　drink 當名詞時指「飲料」，這飲料可以是果汁、可樂、汽水、白開水，但也可以說是酒。如何分辨對方的 drink 指的是什麼，通常從談話的內容可得知。例如：對話一 A 問 Do you want another drink? B 回答 I've enough liquor tonight. 很明顯的看出來當時大家正在喝酒，所以 A 說的 drink 指酒，而 B 拒絕時要強調他酒喝得夠多了，所以用 liquor 這個字。

　　liquor 是指含有酒精的飲料，也就是酒。但平常說要喝酒，不說 liquor 而用 drink。liquor 只用在特別強調「酒」時才用。例如：酒櫃叫

liquor cabinet 或 liquor closet；說某人很有酒量，我們説他能夠 hold liquor，而不是 hold drink。

平常有人問你要不要 any drink，這裏的 drink 就是指任何飲料了，你可以要可樂、汽水、果汁、白開水，甚至於任何酒類，如啤酒、葡萄酒等。

若有人要邀你去 have a drink，那這個 drink 是指去喝酒。吃飯時問你要不要 a before dinner drink，那是指飯前開胃酒。至於有人問你 Do you drink? 那是在問你會不會喝酒。alcohol 是指 drink 或 liquor 中所含的酒精，不是酒。

drink 飲料

▶ 任何飲料

Can I get you any drink?
（你要喝什麼飲料嗎？）

▶ 酒（名詞）

Let's go have a drink.
（我們去喝酒。）

There is a lot of alcohol in this drink.
（這酒中的酒精成分很高。）

Would you like a before dinner drink?
（你要一杯飯前開胃酒嗎？）

▶ 喝酒（動詞）

Do you drink?
（你會喝酒嗎？）

▶ beer 啤酒

Do you want a beer?
（你要一杯啤酒嗎？）

▶ liquor cabinet, liquor closet 酒櫃

▶ wine 葡萄酒；水果酒

Would you like some wine with your dinner?
（你吃飯時要不要喝點葡萄酒？）

Should we get a white wine?
（我們該要一杯白酒嗎？）

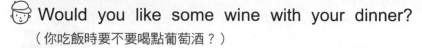
單字片語

- ⊙ liquor ['lɪkə-] 酒
- ⊙ alcohol ['ælkə,hɔl] 酒精
- ⊙ cabinet ['kæbənɪt] 櫃子
- ⊙ closet ['klɑzɪt] 櫃子
- ⊙ bar [bɑr] 酒吧

54 dry town

不准賣酒的城市叫做 dry town

MP3 55

對話

 Would you bring some beers when you come?

（你來時可以帶一些啤酒來嗎？）

My city is a dry town. I have to drive twenty miles to get the beers.

（我們鎮上不賣酒，我要開車開 20 哩才能買到啤酒。）

 Sure. No problem.

（好的，沒問題。）

小秘訣

　說到飲料，正式的英文字是 beverage，這個字指所有的飲料，但不包括白開水。drink 也是飲料的意思，是較常用的字。這兩個字都包含了酒這種飲料。提到酒時，為了避免說不清楚，可以說 alcoholic beverages 或 alcholic drink。

　美國有些城市不准賣酒，這樣的城市叫做 dry town。

 單字片語

- alcoholic [ˌælkəˈhɔlɪk] 酒精的
- beverage [ˈbɛvrɪdʒ] 飲料
- town [taʊn] 城鎮

147

55 formal / casual

要參加宴會前，最好先問清楚是 formal 還是 casual

MP3 56

對話

 Is this dance formal or informal?
（這次的舞會正不正式？）

It is casual.
（是非正式的。）

小秘訣

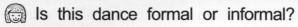

　正式的場合、聚會英文是 formal。非正式的場合、聚會，可以說 informal，也可以用 casual。

formal 正式的

Is the dance formal?
（這次的舞會正式嗎？）

Do not dress up. This is not formal.
（不要盛裝。這是非正式的。）

This is a semi-formal event.
（這是個半正式的場合。）

informal 非正式的

 I'm sorry this meeting is so informal.
（很抱歉這次的會議如此隨便。）

This will be an informal gathering.
（這是一次非正式的聚會。）

▶ casual 非正式的

 The evening will be casual.
（今晚是非正式的。）

 單字片語

- ○ formal [ˈfɔrml̩] 正式的
- ○ casual [ˈkæʒʊəl] 非正式的
- ○ dress up 盛裝
- ○ semi [ˈsɛmɪ] 半

56 formal / official

formal 和 official 都翻譯成正式的，卻有不同的用法

MP3 57

對話

Will I receive official notification of this?
（我會接到正式的通知嗎？）

Yes, we will send it to you in writing.
（會的，我們會書面通知你。）

小秘訣

formal 和 official 中文翻譯都是「正式的」，可是兩個字卻有不同的用法。

Formal 是指一個場合或一個聚會很隆重、很盛大。official 是指一件事情經過當局的認可，不是私底下隨便決定的。

official 公式的；正式的

Is this official?
（這是正式的嗎？）

I am waiting for official confirmation.
（我正等正式的確認。）

I'll need that in writing.
（我需要書面的。）

 單字片語

- ⊘ receive [rɪˈsiv] 接到

- ⊘ notification [ˌnotəfəˈkeʃən] 通知

- ⊘ confirmation [ˌkɑnfɚˈmeʃən] 確認

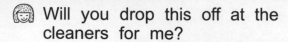

57 cleaners / Laundromat / laundry room

同樣是洗衣服，地方不同英文也不同，別弄錯

MP3 58

對話一

👧 Will you drop this off at the cleaners for me?

（你可以幫我把這個拿去乾洗店嗎？）

🤠 Sure.

（好的。）

對話二

👧 I need to go to the Laundromat.

（我要去自助洗衣店。）

🤠 Me too.

（我也要去。）

小秘訣

　　要拿衣服到洗衣店去洗，這樣的洗衣店英語叫 cleaners。到洗衣店大半是送去乾洗，若要強調乾洗店，可以說 dry cleaners。

　　那種自己投幣自助洗衣的洗衣店，英文叫 laundromat。

　　在美國公寓大樓內大都設有洗衣房，那裏也是自助洗衣，主要是給公寓大樓內的房客使用，英文叫 laundry room。

　　laundry 這個字的意思是洗衣服的地方或是要洗的衣物。

cleaners 洗衣店；乾洗店

 I need to take this to the dry cleaners.
（我需要把這個拿到乾洗店去。）

▶ dry clean 乾洗

I need to have my blouse dry cleaned.
（我的上衣需要拿去乾洗。）

Laundromat 自助洗衣店

 Where is the nearest laundromat?
（最近的自助洗衣店在哪裏？）

▶ laundry room 洗衣房

Does your apartment complex have a laundry room?
（你們的公寓大樓有洗衣房嗎？）

 I left my stuff in the laundry room to dry.
（我把我的東西留在洗衣房晾乾。）

單字片語

- ✪ cleaner [ˈklinɚ] 洗衣店
- ✪ laundromat [ˈlɔndrəˌmæt] 自助洗衣店
- ✪ laundry [ˈlɔndrɪ] 洗衣房
- ✪ dry [draɪ] 乾

the point / What do you mean?

講話要有 point（重點），別人才聽得懂

對話一

 What do you mean?

（你在說什麼？）

 The point I'm trying to make is that you didn't study hard enough.

（我說你還不夠用功。）

對話二

 My point is that if you don't do better work. I'll have to fire you.

（我是說，如果你不做好一點，我會開除你。）

 I understand.

（我知道。）

小秘訣

當你聽不懂對方到底在講什麼，你可以問 What do you mean? 有一個字更好用，就是 point 這個字。point 這個字是重點、主題的意思。有人話講了半天，叫人摸不著邊際，你可以告訴他 Get to the point. 或 What is your point? 意思是你到底要說什麼，直接講清楚，不要拉雜一堆，不知所云。

你如果要直接了當的告訴對方你要說什麼，可以用 My point is ～，或 The point I'm trying to make is ～來起頭。

point 重點，主題

What is your point?
（你到底要說什麼？）

Get to the point.
（把你的用意講出來。）

I don't understand what your point is.
（我不知道你想說什麼。）

▶ 其他說法

What I'm trying to say is don't jump into conclusion.
（我要說的就是別妄下結論。）

What are you getting at?
（你要說什麼？）

What are you trying to say?
（你想說什麼？）

What are you saying?
（你在說什麼？）

 單字片語

- point [pɔɪnt] 重點
- conclusion [kən'kluʒən] 結論
- jump into conclusion 妄下結論
- fire [faɪr] v. 開除

155

59 fix

fix 可以是 fix 早餐，也可以是 fix 一個收音機，可別會錯意

MP3 60

對話一

🎧 My radio is broken.
（我的收音機壞了。）

🤠 Let me look at it.
（讓我看看。）

🎧 Can you repair it?
（你可以修好嗎？）

🤠 I'll fix it if I can.
（如果能夠的話，我會把它修好。）

對話二

🎧 Will you fix dinner tonight?
（今晚你可以幫我弄晚餐嗎？）

🤠 I can't. I've got to work.
（不行，我要去上班。）

小秘訣

　　fix 有兩種不同的意思，注意看句中的意思，別搞混了。有人請你幫他 fix dinner，是想請你幫他弄一份晚餐，可不是晚餐壞了請你把它修理好。fix 若當弄晚餐，或弄一杯飲料時，用法與 make 相同。

　　fix 也可當「修理壞掉的東西」，這種用法與 repair 用法一樣。

fix 修理

I can fix your TV for you.
（我可以幫你修好你的電視。）

My roof needs fixing.
（我的屋頂需要修理。）

Are you good at fixing things?
（你很會修理東西嗎？）

If it's not broken, don't fix it.
（如果沒壞的話，別修理它。）

▶ repair 修理

Do you know of a good car repair shop?
（你知不知道有哪家好的修車廠？）

This VCR is in need of repair.
（這個錄影機需要修理。）

He is repairing my bike.
（他正在修理我的腳踏車。）

It was beyond repair.
（它不能修理了。）

fix 準備（餐點或飲料）

Will you fix me a sandwich?
（你可以幫我做一份三明治嗎？）

Fix me a drink.
（幫我弄杯飲料。）

▶ make 準備（餐點或飲料）

Would you make me a drink?
（你可以為我準備一份飲料嗎？）

I'll make you a sandwich in a minute.
（我馬上替你準備一份三明治。）

 單字片語

- broken ['brokən] 壞了
- repair [rɪ'pɛr] 修理
- beyond repair 無法修理
- be good at ～ 很會做～

60 wash the dishes

美國人飯後是要 wash the dishes，不是 wash the bowls

MP3 61

對話一

It's your turn to wash the dishes.
（輪到你洗碗了。）

No, it's not. I fixed dinner.
（不，才不是呢，我煮了晚飯了。）

You still have to do the dishes.
（你還是要洗碗。）

All right.
（好吧。）

對話二

I don't mind cooking, but I hate doing dishes.
（我不介意煮飯，但我不喜歡洗碗。）

Me too.
（我也是。）

　　中、英文的差異，有些是起因於中、美文化的差異，有些說法你就是不能由中文直接翻譯成英文。例如說到洗碗，你告訴美國人我要去 wash the bowls，對方可能要想很久，才會聽懂你想做什麼。有時候可能還會誤會你是要去洗廁所呢。

　　wash the bowls 從文法上來說沒有錯，中國人吃飯都是用碗，吃完飯去 wash the bowls 是很自然的事；奈何美國人吃飯都是用 dishes，喝湯是用深一點的 dishes。所以他們一聽到 wash the dishes 就很順耳，因為他們都是這麼說的。既然是人家的語言，何不入境隨俗，說 wash the dishes 這樣道地的英語呢？

　　wash the dishes，也可以說 do the dishes。

wash the dishes 洗碗

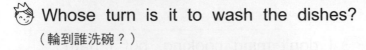 Whose turn is it to wash the dishes?
（輪到誰洗碗？）

If we can't pay for our dinner, we may wind up washing dishes.
（如果我們沒錢付晚飯錢，可得留下來洗碗了。）

You wash the dishes and I'll dry them.
（你洗碗，我來擦乾。）

▶ do the dishes 洗碗

I don't want to do the dishes.
（我不要洗碗。）

Will you help me do the dishes?
（你可以幫我洗碗嗎？）

 I have already done the dishes.
（我把碗洗好了。）

61 water the plants

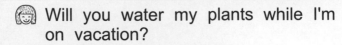

美國人不說澆花，卻說 water the plants（植物）

MP3 62

對話一

 Will you water my plants while I'm on vacation?

（我去度假時，你可以幫我澆花嗎？）

Sure.

（當然可以。）

 Great, just water them twice a week.

（很好，只要一星期澆兩次水就行了。）

Do they need to sit in the sunshine?

（他們需要放在陽光下嗎？）

對話二

 I forgot to water my plants last week.

（我上星期忘了澆花。）

Oh, no, did they die?

（噢，不好了，那些花死了沒有？）

小秘訣

　　跟洗碗一樣，中國人說澆花 water the flowers，美國人卻說 water the plants。當然你也可以堅持說 water the flowers，但美國朋友就會認為你的英語很破。直譯式英語，只是在告訴你的美國朋友你不會說道地的美國話；就像英語 water the plants，如果有外國朋友硬要翻譯成澆植物，老中聽來也會覺得奇怪。

water the plants 澆花

I keep forgetting to water my plants.
（我總是忘記澆我的那些植物。）

I water my plants, but I still can't keep them alive.
（我的植物澆水了，但還是活不了。）

▶ water 澆水

How much water should I give my plants?
（我的植物要澆多少水？）

Be careful not to over water your plants.
（別澆太多水。）

This poor plant needs more water.
（這些植物需要多一點的水。）

This plant is thirsty.
（這個植物需要水。）

163

I don't want to drown my plant.
（我不想把我的植物淹死。）

 Give it plenty of water.
（給它很多的水。）

 單字片語

- ⊙ sunshine [ˈsʌnˌʃaɪn] 陽光

- ⊙ thirsty [ˈθɝstɪ] 口渴

- ⊙ drown [draʊn] 淹死

62 in my day / in those days

我們那時候，英文不是說 in our days

對話一

😊 Mary asked Tom out on a date.

（瑪麗約湯姆出去約會。）

🤠 In my day, girls didn't ask the boys out.

（我們那時候，女孩子不約男孩子出去的。）

😊 Well, times are changing.

（時代在變。）

🤠 Indeed.

（是啊！）

對話二

😊 What did people do for entertainment before television?

（有電視以前，人們做什麼消遣？）

🤠 In those days, people read and held conversations.

（那時候，人們看書或是一起聊天。）

　　人們常喜歡說我們那時候如何如何，英文不說 in our days，而是說 in my day。但若提到以前的時代，說那時候如何如何時，則要用複數的型態 in those days，或 in the old days。

　　說到時代在變，也是用複數形 Times are changing.。

in my day 我們那時候

That was unheard of in my day.
（那種事在我們那時候沒聽過。）

In my day, there wasn't much crime.
（我們那時候，沒有很多犯罪。）

In my day, Coca Colas cost a nickel.
（我們那時候，可口可樂只要五分錢。）

in those days 在那時候

In those days, we all wore the same clothes.
（在那時候，我們都穿相同的衣服。）

▶ in the old days 在從前

In the old days, people were friendlier.
（在從前，人們比較友善。）

In the old days, you didn't have to worry about theft.

（在從前，你不用擔心偷竊。）

times are changing 時代在變

Times are changing. We have to change, too.

（時代在變，我們也要變。）

The times have changed, but not for the better.

（時代是變了，但並沒有變好。）

 單字片語

- ⊕ entertainment [‚ɛntəˈtenmənt]　娛樂
- ⊕ conversation [‚kɑnvəˈseʃən]　會話
- ⊕ crime [kraɪm] 犯罪
- ⊕ nickel [ˈnɪkl̩] 五分錢
- ⊕ theft [θɛft] 偷竊

63 album / CD / tape

要聽音樂，有 album、CD 和 tape 可以選擇

MP3 64

對話一

🎧 Do you have any albums?
（你有唱片嗎？）

🤠 No, I only have CDs.
（沒有，我只有 CD。）

🎧 Have you got any Rolling Stones?
（你有沒有滾石合唱團的？）

🤠 Of course.
（當然有。）

對話二

🎧 Do you have this song on cassette?
（這首歌卡帶上有沒有？）

🤠 Yes, would you like to hear it?
（有，你要聽嗎？）

小秘訣

　　音樂歌曲以前最常見的出版方式是唱片 (record)、光碟 (CD) 和錄音帶 (tape)。record，也叫做 album 或 record album。tape 和 album 已被 CD 全面取代。現代人更多是從 YOU TUBE 聽歌，或從 iTune 下載歌曲從手機及平板等設備收聽音樂。

album 唱片

▶ record album 唱片

He has a bunch of old record albums.
（他有許多舊唱片。）

▶ record 唱片

Mary played a record on the phonograph.
（瑪麗在留聲機上放唱片。）

▶ CD 光碟

I have a large CD collection.
（我收集了很多 CD。）

How much did that CD cost?
（那片 CD 要多少錢？）

CDs are too expensive.
（CD 太貴了。）

▶ cassette tape 錄音帶（卡帶）

I lost my favorite cassette tape.
（我丟了我最喜歡的錄音帶。）

Have you seen my Eagles tape?
（你有沒有看見我的老鷹合唱團的錄音帶？）

 I need the tape you borrowed back.

（我要你還我借你的錄音帶。）

 In my day, we listened to 8 track tapes.

（我們那時候都是聽八聲道錄音帶。）

 單字片語

- ✿ bunch [bʌntʃ] 一束；一串
- ✿ a bunch of 許多
- ✿ favorite ['fevrɪt] 最喜愛的
- ✿ record [rɪˈkɔrd] 唱片
- ✿ phonograph ['fonəˌgræf] 留聲機
- ✿ collection [kəˈlɛkʃən] 收集

64 album

album 有很多意思，要視情況決定

小秘訣

album 原來的意思是一本空白的簿子，可以放相片、郵票。因為唱片 (record) 也是放進一個封套內，所以也叫 album。當有人說到 album 時，可能指唱片、相簿、或集郵簿。到底指那一樣，完全看說話當時的情況而定。

album 用得最多的意思是指相簿。尤其是現在幾乎很少看到唱片，提到 (album) 的機會更少。所以說到相簿時，儘管說 album 就行，不必特別強調 photo album。

record album 唱片

 He has a bunch of old record albums.

（他有許多舊唱片。）

We gave Mary an album by her favorite singer for her birthday.

（在瑪麗生日時，我們送她最喜歡的歌星唱片。）

▶ photo album 相簿

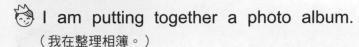 I am putting together a photo album.

（我在整理相簿。）

Do you have any pictures for the album?

（你有沒有相片可以放在相簿內？）

▶ stamp album 集郵簿

She kept her collection of stamps in the albums.

（她把她收集的郵票放在集郵簿內。）

 單字片語

- ✪ album ['ælbəm] 相簿；集郵簿；唱片

- ✪ photo ['foto] 相片

- ✪ singer ['sɪŋɚ] 歌手

- ✪ stamp [stæmp] 郵票

65 tape

tape 也有很多意思，要看說話時的況去分辨是哪一種 tape

對話

Mom, did you see my tape?

（媽，你有沒有看到我的帶子？）

I put it on the TV cabinet.

（我把它放在電視櫃裏。）

No, I didn't mean the VCR tape.

（不，我不是說錄影機的帶子。）

I meant the cassette tape with all my favorite songs.

（我是說我最喜歡的歌曲卡帶。）

Oh, that tape. I'm sorry I didn't see it.

（噢，那個帶子。很抱歉我沒有看到。）

小秘訣

　　tape 這個字可以指錄影帶、錄音帶或是膠帶。如何分辨是指哪種東西，要看說話當時的情況而定。當有人說要把節目錄下來，或有人正在看電視，大聲叫你來看 tape 時，一定是指錄影帶。當有人要你聽 tape 裏的歌，那時的 tape 就是錄音帶。有人要包包裹或是黏東

西時說的 tape，一定是膠帶了。

對話的例句是很常見的美國家庭對話，千萬別因為可能有那樣的誤會，而非要強調VCR tape（錄影帶）、cassette tape（錄音帶）不行，那會使你的英語聽起來很不自然。要強調 VCR tape、cassette tape 或是 Scotch tape，只有在對方不清楚你要哪一種 tape，必須特別說明時才用。

叫人來看 tape，只要說 Come watch this tape for a minute. 就行，別說 Come watch this VCR tape for a minute.。

tape 帶子

▶ VCR tape 錄影帶

Do you have any blank tape I can use to record the program?
（你有沒有空白錄影帶，我可以用來錄這個節目？）

Come watch this tape for a minute.
（來看一下這帶子的節目。）

▶ cassette tape 錄音帶（卡帶）

Listen to the tape. Isn't the song wonderful?
（聽聽看這錄音帶，這首歌是不是很棒？）

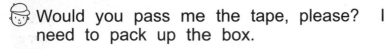

▶ Scotch tape 膠帶

Would you pass me the tape, please? I need to pack up the box.

（可以把膠帶遞給我嗎？我要打包這個盒子。）

 單字片語

- blank [blæŋk] 空白的

- program ['progræm] 節目

- pass [pæs] 遞過來

- pack [pæk] 打包

66 in the morning / in an hour

in the morning 到底是明天早上，還是今天早上

MP3 67

對話一

 You need to take the trash out.
（你必須把垃圾拿出去。）

 I will.
（我會的。）

 When?
（什麼時候？）

 I'll do it in the morning.
（我明天早上會做。）

對話二

 When is your trip?
（你何時要去旅行？）

 I am leaving in two weeks.
（兩個星期之後要走。）

小秘訣

　　還記得中學英文老師說 in the morning 是指「早上的時間」吧？那這個美國人難道是說「我只在早上的時間才做事」？其實這是中英文語法上的差異，他是說「我明天早上做」。既然是明天早上，為什麼不說 tomorrow morning 呢？注意了，in the morning 有明天一早的意思，要是有客戶請你幫他做事，你用中國式英語回答 I'll do it tomorrow morning.「我要等到明天早上才做」，就太怠慢客戶了！不可不謹慎啊。

當美國朋友問你何時要去旅行時，你若是兩個星期之後要走，千萬別說 after two weeks。要記住中文說一小時之後、兩星期之後、一個月之後，英文要用 in an hour, in two weeks, in a month。

in an hour 一小時之後

I'll be there in an hour.
（我一小時之後會到那裏。）

I'll get that information to you in a little bit.
（等一下我會把那消息給你。）

I'll turn the TV off in a little while.
（我等一會兒會把電視關掉。）

in the morning 明天早上

She will call you in the morning.
（她明天早上會打電話給你。）

Let me know in the morning.
（明天早上告訴我。）

I'll do it first thing in the morning.
（明天早上我第一件事就是做這件事。）

 單字片語

- trash [træʃ] 垃圾

- turn off 關掉

- information [ˌɪnfɚˈmeʃən] 消息；資訊

67 near-sighted / far-sighted / 20 / 20 vision

20/20 **vision** 是正常視力，沒近視也沒遠視

MP3
68

對話一

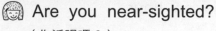 Are you near-sighted?

（你近視嗎？）

No, I am far-sighted.

（不，我是遠視。）

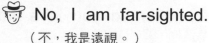 What does that mean?

（那是什麼意思？）

It means I can see far away, but not up close.

（那是說我可以看清遠方，但近物就看不清楚。）

對話二

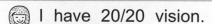 I have 20/20 vision.

（我的視力是 20/20。）

Wow, that's perfect vision.

（哇，那是標準視力。）

小秘訣

我們常認為沒有近視就代表視力很標準。實際上，標準視力應該是沒近視也沒遠視。所以英語說視力很好，或是沒有近視，要說 I have 20/20 vision. 或是 I have perfect vision. 千萬別說 I don't have near-Sighted.。

178

near-sighted 近視

 Are you near-sighted?

（你有近視嗎？）

▶ far-sighted 遠視

▶ 20/20 vision 視力標準

 I have 20/20 vision.

（我的視力很標準。）（我沒有近視。）

 I have perfect vision.

（我的視力很標準。）（我沒有近視。）

 單字片語

- ○ near-sighted [nɪr'saɪtɪd] 近視
- ○ far-sighted [far'saɪtɪd] 遠視
- ○ vision ['vɪʒən] 視力
- ○ perfect ['pɝfɪkt] 十全十美的

68 power / prescription

近視的度數是 power 不是 degree

MP3
69

小秘訣

我們常會問別人「你近視幾度?」,不是問他眼鏡的 degree,而是要問他眼鏡的 power,有時也會問他眼鏡的 prescription(處方)。在美國配眼鏡,一定要有眼科醫生驗光後給的 prescription 才可以配眼鏡。處方上有眼鏡該配的度數。

也可以問眼鏡有多 strong(深)。

power (眼鏡的)度數

What's the power of your glasses?
(你的眼鏡幾度?)

▶ prescription (眼鏡的)處方

What prescription do you wear?
(你近視幾度?)

▶ strong (近視)深

How strong are your glasses?
(你近視幾度?)

單字片語

- power [ˈpauɚ]（眼鏡的）度數
- prescription [prɪˈskrɪpʃən] 處方
- glasses [glæs] 眼鏡
- wear [wɛr] 戴

69 glasses / contacts

隱形眼鏡，英語不可直接翻譯成 invisible

MP3
70

對話一

Where are your glasses?
（你的眼鏡呢？）

I don't need them anymore.
（我不需要它們了。）

Why not?
（為什麼？）

Because I got contact lenses.
（因為我配了隱形眼鏡。）

對話二

Are you wearing your contacts today?
（你今天有戴隱形眼鏡嗎？）

No, I lost one of them.
（沒有，我丟了其中一個。）

小秘訣

　　隱形眼鏡不是直接翻譯成 invisible glasses，應該是（接觸鏡片）contact lenses。contact 是接觸，lens 是鏡片。隱形眼鏡是把鏡片 (lens) 直接放在眼球上，所以是接觸眼球的鏡片。

普通眼鏡一定有兩個玻璃鏡片，所以要用玻璃 (glass) 的複數形 glasses。

隱形眼鏡的全名是 contact lenses，簡單說成 contacts 也行。隱形眼鏡是左、右各一個 lens，所以不像 glasses 永遠是複數形。有時說到其中一個時，也可說 a contact 或 a contact lens。

老花眼鏡是老年人看近物、看書時要戴的眼鏡，英文叫做 reading glasses。

contact lenses 隱形眼鏡

Oh no, I lost a contact.
（噢，不，我丟了一個隱形眼鏡。）

I ripped a contact lens.
（我弄破了一個隱形眼鏡。）

Are those colored contacts?
（那是有色的隱形眼鏡嗎？）

I can't sleep in my contacts.
（戴著隱形眼鏡，我不能睡。）

▶ glasses 眼鏡

You have strong glasses.
（你的眼鏡度數很深。）

What prescription are your glasses?
（你近視幾度？）

👦 You look good with glasses.
（你戴眼鏡很好看。）

👦 You look different with glasses.
（你戴眼鏡看起來不一樣。）

👦 How long have you had those glasses?
（你有那付眼鏡多久了？）

▶ reading glasses 老花眼鏡

👦 I need reading glasses to read.
（我看書時需要老花眼鏡。）

▶ frame 鏡框

👦 Those frames are really old-fashioned.
（那些鏡框真的太老式了。）

 單字片語

- contact ['kɑntækt] 接觸
- lens [lɛnz] 鏡片；(複數形)lenses
- glasses [glæsɪz]　眼鏡
- rip [rɪp] 扯裂

70

answer the phone / answer the door

接電話或應門，英語都是用 answer

MP3
71

對話一

🧑 Will you answer the phone?
（你接電話好嗎？）

🤠 I can't get to it.
（我不能接。）

對話二

🧑 Is that the doorbell?
（是門鈴聲嗎？）

🤠 I think so.
（我想是。）

🧑 Will you answer the door?
（你去應門好嗎？）

🤠 Sure.
（好的。）

對話三

🧑 Someone is knocking on the door.
（有人在敲門。）

🤠 I'll get it.
（我去開。）

接電話的英語是 answer the phone，應門的英語是 answer the door，當電話鈴響或有人按門鈴時，你要去接電話或應門，口語上都說 I'll get it.（我去接，或我去開門。）

answer the phone 接電話

Whoever it was hung up when I answered the phone.

（不知道是誰，我接電話時已掛斷了。）

Will someone please answer the phone?

（有誰要接電話？）

answer the door 應門

Will you answer the door?

（你去應門好嗎？）

Go answer the door and see who it is.

（去應門，看看是誰。）

▶ ring 鈴響

The doorbell is ringing.

（門鈴在響著。）

The phone is ringing.
（電話正響著。）

 單字片語

- doorbell [ˈdorbɛl] 門鈴
- knock [nɑk] 敲（門）
- hang up 掛斷（電話）
- ring [rɪŋ]（鈴）響

71 drive-in / drive-thru

drive-in 和 drive-thru 都是免下車，只要把車窗搖下來就可把事辦妥

MP3
72

對話一

🧑 Do you want to eat inside?

（你要進去裏面吃嗎？）

🤠 No, let's go through the drive-thru.

（不要，我們在外賣窗口買了就走。）

🧑 Okay, but I'll need a minute to see what I want.

（好，但我需要一些時間看看我要什麼。）

🤠 That's fine.

（好的。）

對話二

🧑 Would you like to go to the drive-in movies with me?

（你要跟我去看汽車電影嗎？）

🤠 Yes, that would be nice.

（好啊，我想應該不錯。）

188

drive-thru 是 drive-through 的簡寫。

drive-in 和 drive-thru 都是為了方便顧客不要下車，就可以辦妥事情，這都是汽車時代的產物。這兩者的性質有點不同：drive-thru 大部分是用來説餐廳，當你不想進餐廳內用餐，只想外賣帶走時，你就可以到餐廳的外賣窗口買了帶走。

drive-in 是用在銀行、戲院或餐廳，drive-in movie 就是在汽車內看電影。這種 drive-in 戲院大都建在郊區，有很大的銀幕，佔地很大，可同時容納幾十輛汽車停在一起看電影。

drive-in 餐廳是車子停在停車場，餐廳服務生直接到你的車旁點餐，再把餐點送到車上。drive-in 銀行也是不用下車，銀行的收納員透過麥克風和輸送帶，就可以為顧客服務。

drive-through 外賣窗口

Pull up to the drive-through.
（把車子開到外賣窗口。）

Are we going to eat in or drive-through?
（我們要進去裏面吃還是要外賣帶走？）

drive-in 免下車

▶ 汽車電影

We're going to the drive-in this weekend.
（我們這個週末要去看汽車電影。）

Do you have to have a car to go to the drive-in?
（是不是一定要有車子才可以去看汽車電影？）

▶ 免下車餐廳

I'm going to the restaurant that has drive-in.
（我要去免下車餐廳。）

Let's go to the drive-in to get a hamburger.
（我們到免下車餐廳去買個漢堡。）

▶ 免下車銀行

I'll cash the check at the drive-in.
（我要到免下車銀行去兌現這張支票換。）

 單字片語

- through [θru] 通過
- pull up to ～ 停到～

72 lose weight / overweight

減肥或過胖不可以照字面翻譯，注意如何使用 weight 這個字

MP3 73

對話一

👧 Do you think I need to lose weight?
（你認為我該減肥嗎？）

🤠 No, you are not overweight at all.
（不，你一點都不胖。）

👧 No, but my clothes would fit better.
（是不會，但我穿起衣服來會好看些。）

🤠 Then do it.
（那就減肥吧！）

對話二

👧 I need to lose a few pounds.
（我需要減肥幾磅。）

🤠 No, you look good now.
（不，你現在很好看。）

小秘訣

　　當你覺得太胖要減肥時，英文有幾個說法都可以用。可以說 I need to lose weight. I need to lose a few pounds.，或是 I need to go on a diet.。

　　說某人很胖，可以用 fat 這個字，但美國人較常用 overweight 這個字。

lose weight 減肥

You look like you've lost weight.
（你好像瘦了。）

Have you lost weight?
（你瘦了嗎？）

I can't believe you've lost 20 pounds in a month.
（我不敢相信你在一個月內瘦了 20 磅。）

I just want to drop 10 pounds before summer.
（我只想在夏天之前減肥 10 磅。）

► go on a diet 節食

I'm getting too heavy. I'll have to go on a diet.
（我太胖了，我必須要節食。）

overweight 太胖

She is really overweight.
（她真的太胖了。）

 單字片語

- **weight** [wet] 體重

- **overweight** [ˈovɚˌwet] 超重的；太胖的

- **pound** [paʊnd] 磅

- **diet** [ˈdaɪət] 飲食

73 How much do you weigh?

問別人體重要怎麼說

MP3
74

小秘訣

　　問別人的體重多少，可以用動詞 weigh，句型是 How much do (does)+ 主詞 +weigh?，或用名詞 weight，句型是 What's（某人的）weight?

　　回答體重是多少，可以用動詞 weigh，句型是主詞 +weigh(s)+ 磅數（公斤）。或用名詞 weight，句型是（某人的）weight is+ 磅數（公斤）。請看下面的例句。

weigh 重（多少）

How much do you weigh?
（你的體重是多少？）

He weighs 180 pounds.
（他重 180 磅。）

▶ weight 體重

What's your weight?
（你重多少？）

193

Her weight is 50 kilograms.
（她重 50 公斤。）

gain weight 胖了；增加體重

 I've gained 5 pounds in a month.
（我一個月內胖了 5 磅。）

 單字片語

- ☺ weigh [we] 重（多少）

- ☺ kilogram [ˈkɪləˌgræm] 公斤

74

gain weight/put on weight

長胖了，也可以用 weight 這個字

MP3 75

小秘訣

　　英文要注意 weight 這個字用法，我們說某人胖了可以說 be getting fat，但更常見的說法是 gain weight 或是 put on weight，說 be getting heavy 也可以。

put on weight 胖了；體重增加

I have to go on a diet because I've been putting on weight lately.
（我必須節食，因我最近胖了。）

▶ fat 胖

He is getting fat.
（他胖了。）

You are growing fat lately.　You'd better watch your diet.
（你最近胖了，你最好注意你的飲食。）

Does this dress make me look fat?
（這件洋裝是不是讓我看起來比較胖？）

▶ heavy 重

 I'm getting too heavy.
（我胖了。）

 單字片語

- lately [ˈletlɪ] 最近

- heavy [ˈhɛvɪ] 重的

75 How tall are you?

問別人身高多少要怎麼說

MP3
76

對話一

 How tall are you?

（你有多高？）

 6'4".

（6 呎 4 吋。）

 You make me feel so short.

（你讓我覺得我很矮。）

 You're not short.

（你一點也不矮。）

對話二

 I wish I looked like him.

（我希望我像他。）

 He is so tall.

（他好高。）

小秘訣

　　問身高有兩種問法：一種是用形容詞 tall，句型是 How tall+be 動詞 + 主詞？；另一種是用名詞 height，句型是 What is（某人的）height？

　　回答身高多少句型是：主詞 +be 動詞 + 公分（幾呎幾吋），或是（某人的）height is 公分（幾呎幾吋）。

197

How tall are you? 你有多高？

▶ 回答

I am 160 centimeters tall.
（我 160 公分高。）

My sister is five feet tall.
（我的妹妹是 5 呎高。）

He is 6 feet 3 inches.
（他身高 6 呎 3 吋。）

▶ 用 height

What is your height?
（你有多高？）

My height is 180 centimeters.
（我身高 180 公分。）

Mary's height is 5 feet 2 inches.
（瑪麗的身高是 5 呎 2 吋。）

 單字片語

- height [haɪt] 身高

- centimeter [ˈsɛntəˌmitɚ] 公分

She is tall. / She is short.

用 tall 或 short 來說人的高、矮

小秘訣

說到人的高、矮，高用 tall，矮用 short。

tall 高

My whole family are tall.
（我的家人都很高。）

I want to be tall.
（我希望高一點。）

He is such a tall person.
（他長得好高。）

I'll bet he can touch the ceiling.
（我打賭他摸得到天花板。）

short 矮

He is really short.
（他真的很矮。）

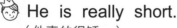

單字片語

○ touch [tʌtʃ] 觸摸　　　　ceiling ['silɪŋ] 天花板

77 ride / drive

ride 是乘、坐；drive 是自己開車

MP3
78

對話一

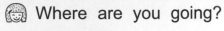 Where are you going?

（你要去哪裏？）

For a drive.

（開車出去兜風。）

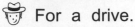 Can I come?

（我可以一起去嗎？）

Sure, but I'm driving.

（可以，但是我要開車。）

對話二

I'm going to the desert.

（我要到沙漠去。）

Wow, that's a long drive.

（哇，那要好遠。）

小秘訣

　　drive 和 ride 都可以當動詞或名詞。當動詞時：drive 是指駕駛（車子）或是開車載（人）；ride 是指搭乘（車、船），例如：ride the bus；ride the train，或是騎（馬、腳踏車、摩托車等），例如：ride the horse, ride the motorcycle。

200

當名詞時；drive 是指開車出遊；ride 是乘、坐的意思。

注意：drive 做載（人）的用法時，一定要有一個地點當副詞，例如 My friend drove me here.（我朋友開車載我來這裡。）或 I drove Mary home.（我開車載瑪麗回家。），千萬別說 My friend drove me.（我的朋友開車載我。），這種說法會讓美國朋友忍不住想回你一句 "That drove me crazy."（真令我受不了！）。

drive 駕車出遊

I'm going for a drive in my new car.
（我要開我的新車去兜風。）

How long of a drive is it?
（開車要多久？）

I want to go for a drive in the country.
（我要到鄉下去兜風。）

▶ 開車（載）；開（車）

Who drove you here?
（誰開車載你來這裡？）

Can I drive your car?
（我可以開你的車嗎？）

ride 搭乘（車、船）；騎（馬；腳踏車；摩托車）

I like to ride the bus.
（我喜歡搭公車。）

Who's riding with you to the party?
（誰要跟你坐車去參加宴會？）

He rode his motorcycle to the wedding.
（他騎摩托車來參加婚禮。）

▶ 乘坐車子

I am just along for the ride.
（我只是搭便車兜風。）

Do you want to go for a ride?
（要坐車去兜風嗎？）

 單字片語

- ride [raɪd] 搭乘；乘坐

- drive [draɪv] 駕駛（車、船）

- desert [ˈdɛzɚt] 沙漠

- country [ˈkʌntrɪ] 鄉下

- motorcycle [ˈmotɚˌsaɪkl̩] 摩托車

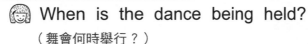

78 be held / be on

on 可以當形容詞，指電影在放映，與動詞 show 意思一樣

MP3
79

對話一

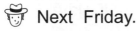 When is the dance being held?

（舞會何時舉行？）

Next Friday.

（下星期五。）

對話二

What time is the movie?

（幾點鐘有電影？）

The movie is on at 5:00, 7:00 and 9:00.

（5 點、7 點和 9 點都有電影。）

Let's go to the 7 o'clock showing.

（我們去看 7 點那一場。）

Sounds good.

（好。）

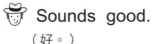 小秘訣

　　電影正在放映可以用 on 或是 show。在幾點放映用介系詞 at。所以説電影在 5 點放映，句子是 The movie is on at 5:00.。注意這句話中的 on 是形容詞，指電影在放映，而 at 是時間之前的介系詞。你也

可以說 The movie is showing at 5:00.。

　　have 當舉行的意思，與 hold 的用法一樣，可以用現在進行式表示未來的事件。

hold 舉行

 When are you holding your garage sale?
（你的車庫賣舊物是什麼時候？）

When is the carnival at school being held?
（學校的園遊會何時舉行？）

We will be holding an auction next week.
（我們下星期有一場拍賣會。）

have 舉行

They are having a party tonight.
（他們今晚有宴會。）

 單字片語

- show [ʃo]　放映
- auction [ˈɔkʃən]　拍賣會

79 dance / ball

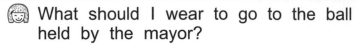

參加 ball 一定要盛裝打扮才行，參加 dance 就不一定

**MP3
80**

對話

 What should I wear to go to the ball held by the mayor?

（我應該穿什麼去參加市長的舞會？）

You should dress up to go to a ball.

（你應該盛裝打扮再去。）

小秘訣

　　dance 是一般的舞會，可以穿得輕鬆些，主要是大家一起跳舞、玩樂，不是很正式，。ball 是一種很盛大、正式的舞會，古代宮庭中的舞會應該叫 ball，絕對不是 dance。

　　Party 是一般的宴會，大家聚在一起聊天、吃東西，也可以跳舞，但跳舞不是 party 的主要目的。以跳舞為主的聚會應該是 dance。

dance 跳舞（舞會）

John and I went to a dance last night.
（約翰和我昨晚去跳舞。）

Would you like to go to the dance with me?
（你要和我去跳舞嗎？）

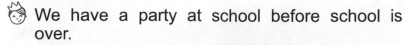

► party 宴會

We have a party at school before school is over.
（學期結束之前，我們舉行了一個宴會。）

We've having a party this Friday. Would you like to come?
（這個星期五我們有個宴會，你要來嗎？）

ball 舞會

The ball held at Polo club was magnificent.
（在馬球俱樂部舉行的舞會很華麗。）

 單字片語

- magnificent [mægˈnɪfəsn̩t] 華麗的
- mayor [ˈmeɚ] 市長
- dress up 盛裝打扮

80 be impressed / impress someone

要給人留下深刻的印象，要很特別才行

對話一

 Do you like my new hairdo?

（你喜歡我的新髮型嗎？）

I am impressed.

（我對它印象深刻。）

對話二

What is wrong with Robert?

（羅勃怎麼啦？）

He has a crush on Mary.

（他愛上了瑪麗。）

Oh, is he trying to impress her?

（噢，他正想辦法引起她的注意嗎？）

Yes, but he's not succeeding.

（是的，但是並不成功。）

小秘訣

　　I'm impressed. 除了字面上「我留下深刻印象」的意思外，還有誇獎的意思在，指某件事很特別，令你記憶深刻。如果你對某事的評語是 I'm not impressed. 那表示你認為它不好，所以沒有留下深刻的印

象。所以 impressive 這個字，也就是用來形容某人或某事很特別，會給別人留下深刻的印象。

be impressed 對～印象深刻

I am really impressed by your knowledge.
（我對你的博學印象深刻。）

Wow, I'm impressed.
（哇，我覺得很特別。）

I am not impressed.
（我並不認為有什麼特殊。）

▶ impress 使人印象深刻

You are not impressing me.
（你並沒有給我特別的印象。）

Cool clothes do not impress me at all.
（我一點也不欣賞耍酷的服裝。）

He is trying to impress her.
（他正想辦法引起她的注意。）

▶ impressive 有深刻印象的

He is an impressive person.
（他是個令人印象深刻的人。）

She is a very impressive woman.
（她是個會給人留下印象的女人。）

▶ impression 印象

You didn't make a good first impression.
（你沒有給人好的第一印象。）

 單字片語

- hairdo [ˈhɛrdu] 髮型；髮式

- impress [ɪmˈprɛs] 留下深刻印象

- impressive [ɪmˈprɛsɪv] 有深刻印象的

- impression [ɪmˈprɛʃən] 印象

81 prep school / trade school

prep school 是預備升大學的學校；trade school 是
準備就業的學校

MP3 82

對話一

Where did you go to high school?
（你上哪一家高中？）

I went to a prep school.
（我上一所大學預備學校。）

So did I.
（我也是。）

Was it co-ed or just for girls?
（你們學校是男、女合校，還是女校？）

It was just for girls.
（是女校。）

Mine was co-ed.
（我們學校是男、女合校。）

對話二

Where did you learn to fix cars?
（你在哪裏學會修車的？）

I learned it in trade school.
（我在職業學校學的。）

小秘訣

　　prep 是 preparatory 的簡寫，是預備的意思。prep school 是一種專門準備升大學的私立學校，這種學校收費昂貴，課程較一般公立高中困難，有貴族學校的味道。

　　trade school 類似台灣的職業學校，學校的課程以訓練就業技能為主。

prep school 大學預備學校

Prep school was harder than college.
（大學預備學校比大學還難。）

My parents sent me to prep school to get me ready for college.
（我的父母送我到大學預備學校，準備上大學。）

I went to a prep school.
（我上大學預備學校。）

He went to the best preparatory school in the Southwest.
（他上西南區最好的大學預備學校。）

trade school 職業學校

I went to a trade school for beauticians.
（我上職業學校學做美容師。）

Did you learn that skill in trade school?
（你在職業學校學那項技能的嗎？）

Working on electronics is only one skill I learned in trade school.
（電子是我在職業學校學到的唯一技能。）

▶ trade 職業

Maybe you should forget about college and learn a trade instead.
（或許你不要想上大學，去學一樣職業技能吧。）

 單字片語

- prep [prɛp] 預備的
- trade [tred] 職業
- beautician [bjuˈtɪʃən] 美容師
- electronics [ɪˌlɛkˈtrɑnɪks]　電子工學

82 cram school/crash course

crash course 更接近補習班的意思

小秘訣

cram 這個字是指考前開夜車、猛K書的意思。台灣的補習班若翻譯成 cram school，美國人是聽不懂的。即使你向老美解釋台灣教育的情況後，美國人也絕不會同意補習班叫 cram school 的。

crash 這個字有加強課業輔導的意思，你若說你要上 crash course，美國人可以了解你是要去加強課業，那就很接近補習的意思了。如果你要用更白話的英語來說補習，可以說你要去參加 intensive study class。

intensive study class 是指密集加強班，雖然不是跟台灣補習班的形式一樣，但總比用臨時開夜車的 cram 更適當。

cram 臨時開夜車唸書

She spent the night cramming for the test.
（她整晚開夜車唸書。）

If you would study all the time, you wouldn't need to cram.
（如果你平時唸書的話，也不用開夜車了。）

crash course 課業加強班

I'm taking a crash course in math.
（我在上數學的加強班。）

▶ intensive study class 密集加強班

I'm going to an intensive study class for math.
（我要去上數學的密集加強班。）

I'm taking an intensive study courses.
（我在上密集加強班。）

 單字片語

- ✪ cram [kræm] 臨時開夜車唸書
- ✪ crash [kræʃ] 加強課業
- ✪ intensive [ɪnˈtɛnsɪv] 密集的

It's getting late. / It's dark. / It's still bright.

很晚了，但不一定天黑了

MP3 84

對話一

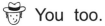 It's getting late.
（很晚了。）

I've got to run.
（我該走了。）

Be careful.
（小心點。）

You too.
（你也一樣。）

對話二

I can't believe it's 9:00 p.m. already.
（我真不相信已經是晚上 9 點了。）

Yes, it's still so bright.
（是啊，天色還很亮。）

小秘訣

　　我們說很晚了是指時間上的晚，用 It's late.。很晚並不表示外面已經天黑了，有時 It's still bright.（天還很亮）；有時 It's dark.（已經天黑了）。

It's dark 天黑了

It's getting dark.
（天漸漸暗了。）

It's really dark out there tonight.
（今晚外面天色很黑。）

I can't see the road it is so dark.
（好暗,我看不到路。）

▶ before dark 天黑以前

I'd better go before dark.
（我最好在天黑之前走。）

▶ after dark 天黑以後

We shouldn't drive long distances after dark.
（天黑以後,我們不應該開長途。）

▶ too late 太晚了

I've got leave before it's too late.
（趁還沒太晚,我該走了。）

 Is it bright when you leave for work?
（你去上班的時候天亮的嗎？）

It's too bright in this room.
（這個房間太亮了。）

 單字片語

- careful ['kɛrfəl] 小心的

- bright [braɪt] 明亮的

- dark [dɑrk] 黑暗的

- distance ['dɪsənts] 距離

- leave [liv] 離開

英語系列：31

3分鐘學會道地英語

作者／張瑪麗
出版者／哈福企業有限公司
地址／新北市中和區景新街 347 號 11 樓之 6
電話／(02) 2945-6285　傳真／(02) 2945-6986
郵政劃撥／31598840　戶名／哈福企業有限公司
出版日期／2016 年 6 月
定價／NT$ 299 元（附 MP3）

全球華文國際市場總代理／采舍國際有限公司
地址／新北市中和區中山路 2 段 366 巷 10 號 3 樓
電話／(02) 8245-8786　傳真／(02) 8245-8718
網址／www.silkbook.com　新絲路華文網

香港澳門總經銷／和平圖書有限公司
地址／香港柴灣嘉業街 12 號百樂門大廈 17 樓
電話／(852) 2804-6687　傳真／(852) 2804-6409
定價／港幣 100 元（附 MP3）

視覺指導／Wan Wan
封面設計／Vi Vi
內文排版／Jo Jo
email／haanet68@Gmail.com

郵撥打九折，郵撥未滿 500 元，酌收 1 成運費，
滿 500 元以上者免運費

國家圖書館出版品預行編目資料

3分鐘學會道地英語 / 張瑪麗 著. -- 初版. -- 新北市：哈
福企業, 2016.06
　　面；　公分. -- (英語系列；31)
　　ISBN 978-986-5616-61-8（平裝附光碟片）

1.英語　2.讀本

805.18　　　　　　　　　　　　　　105007879

哈福